THE LODGE

THE LODGE

CHRIS COPPEL

Matador
9 Priory Business Park,
Wistow Road, Kibworth Beauchamp,
Leicestershire. LE8 0RX
Tel: 0116 279 2299
Email: books@troubador.co.uk
Web: www.troubador.co.uk/matador
Twitter: @matadorbooks

ISBN 978 1800460 072

British Library Cataloguing in Publication Data.
A catalogue record for this book is available from the British Library.

Printed and bound in Great Britain by 4edge Limited
Typeset in 11pt Minion Pro by Troubador Publishing Ltd, Leicester, UK

Matador is an imprint of Troubador Publishing Ltd

CHAPTER
ONE

Constable Andrew Whiting was freezing. The police station was freezing. All of bloody Scotland was freezing.

He hated winter – yet he'd once again returned to a place that was guaranteed to be perpetually cold. For a man who hated the cold, it made no sense. It was like a recovering alcoholic choosing to live above a pub.

When he was a young lad, he'd never imagined that he would one day become a 'copper'. As a child growing up in the suburbs of Inverness the idea of being a policeman back then would have made him laugh. Though to be fair, there was a time when he thought the uniform would look good on him.

The Kingussie posting was his first. He had been the only person graduating who'd requested a position in such a small town in the middle of nowhere. He didn't see it that way. While the other recruits hoped for one of the big cities – Andrew had requested a remote location in the Highlands.

Having just turned twenty-one he was a bit scrawny, but was determined to bulk up and weight train so he could make himself more daunting to the criminal element. As it was, at just over a metre and a half tall and weighing only sixty-two kilos, he needed whatever help he could get.

*

Being stuck on the night shift over the Christmas holidays was the absolute pits. Being stuck in a station house with a dodgy boiler was the icing on the shit cake. When they had re-opened the station house six months earlier, after an eight-year budget closure, they had planned on replacing the heating system. The budget ran out after the roof repairs and getting the station's only toilet to work again.

At least it wasn't one of the days of the year when an all-nighter was required. Hogmanay was the worst. That shift truly was a nightmare. Even the most conscientious and mild-mannered Scot seemed to feel the need to howl at the moon on New Year's Eve. Especially so after half a dozen pints of brown and a few shorts to make the evening special.

Keeping the station manned all night on the 31st was meant to be enough of a deterrent to sway some of the townsfolk from their usual alcohol-induced stupidity.

As it was only the 23rd December they had a much easier go of it, though they still couldn't shut up shop till 9 p.m.

It was a pain, but from the 22nd through New Year's Eve, they kept the tiny station house open beyond the

2

usual 5 p.m. Locals just seemed to drink that bit more on those days. Plus, it's a long-standing Scottish tradition that if you drink more, you fight more.

There were only two constables on duty that night and they took turns on the call-outs. It was gone 8 p.m., so the volume of incidents was thankfully on the decline. The days leading up to Christmas seemed to have the majority of incidents occur earlier in the evening.

Constable Davies was having a kip in the station's only cell. Andrew was on the duty desk.

He was staring at the phone, praying for it to ring. It's not that he wanted to get in the midst of an altercation at the Stag and Hunter or wherever, it's just that the station's only dedicated police car had heating.

Heavenly heating!

They'd run out of tea an hour ago and some prat had buggered off with the instant coffee. A call-out really was the only way Andrew was going to get anywhere close to warm that night. Even when he got off duty, his digs were a badly converted garage with a single thirty-year-old electric bar heater for warmth.

He stared at the old-fashioned Bakelite phone, again willing it to ring. Cold makes you do some pretty stupid things.

As he tried to use his mind to entice the blasted thing to do something – it actually rang, scaring the bejesus out of him.

"Kingussie Police Station." Andrew used his best police-officer voice.

The woman on the other end of the line sounded young. She also sounded very upset.

"Please help! It's awful. One of our guests! He's dead. Please hurry."

Andrew could see on the computer interface that the call was coming from the Waylight B & B, about twenty miles from the police station. Twenty miles straight into the hills beyond Drumguish. Not a pleasant drive in the dark. Even worse as it had started to snow. Lightly now, but it could easily start dumping the stuff in earnest. The weather boys were doing their usual bollocks of predicting the biggest snowfall in decades. They'd say anything to get people glued to the telly.

"Can you tell me what happened?"

"I don't know. We were just…"

The line went dead.

Andrew tried calling back, but could only get the busy tone.

"Bugger!" he mumbled to himself as he headed to wake Davies.

*

The Ford Fiesta warmed up in seconds, finally giving Andrew the heat he so craved. The drive however, was still shite. The road up to the Waylight was the B970. It had no markings and no illumination. The light snow had managed to blanket the narrow road, enough so that it masked where the paved road ended and the berm began.

He knew his only choice was to stick to the middle of the narrow lane, just to be safe. Thankfully, the relatively new Fiesta had LED headlights that actually cut through the dark. Their old car, a clapped-out Focus, did little but send a weak yellow wash about ten feet in front of the bonnet.

The drive took over an hour. Not a single car passed him the whole way. Then again, there wasn't much of anything along that stretch of road anyway. Two farms and the B & B. Bloody desolate as far as Andrew was concerned.

What was troubling was that the light snowfall down in the village was more like a raging blizzard up in the hills. He was driving through at least fifteen centimetres of soft powder and it was becoming a tad perilous. The little Ford was never meant to be driven in those conditions.

He had little choice but to keep going. He shifted to second and kept it there. A mile further on, there was a sharp bend that curved to the right. Andrew knew it was there and kept in the middle of the road and in second gear.

It was a good thing too. The moment he completed the blind curve, he saw a stag standing in the middle of the road blocking his way. It was a beautiful creature, despite being a complete hazard to unsuspecting drivers.

Andrew changed into first gear then slowly pumped his brakes, hoping to avoid a skid. He came to a stop less than a metre from the animal. It looked down at Andrew's tiny police car with utter disinterest. Andrew tried flashing his lights which did exactly nothing. He tried the rooftop police light, again with no results. He thought about using the horn but really didn't want to startle the animal.

He stepped out of the car into heavy powdered snow and slowly approached the stag. It watched him closely but without any sign of fear or concern. Andrew tried waving his arms at it. The majestic creature looked back with an almost bored expression.

Andrew then gently patted its hind quarters. The animal let out a huge plume of nasal condensation, but didn't move a muscle. Andrew then placed both his hands on its rump, with the intention of giving it a good push.

Instead, he felt a wave of energy pass between them. It felt almost like a low-voltage electrical shock. For a microsecond, Andrew saw himself back at the side of the A1(M) motorway off-ramp. He could smell the smoke and the carnage, then it was gone.

The stag turned its head and looked directly into Andrew's eyes. Andrew could have sworn that he saw something behind them. He thought he saw some sort of recognition.

The stag slowly walked off the lane, onto the berm, then walked into the shadowed darkness of the adjacent woods.

Andrew got back in the car. He was about to put it into gear but instead just sat there for a few minutes. He felt momentarily dazed. The sensation passed, and Andrew put the little Ford in gear and continued the drive up the narrow, snow-covered road.

After what seemed like an eternity, he pulled into the drive that led to the Waylight. It took some very creative driving to make it up to the top without getting himself royally stuck!

*

The Waylight had originally been a manor farm. When the owners gave up trying to make a decent living off the place, they decided to at least try to recoup a few quid by letting it. They were able to get a small income from the property but there was a lot of tenant turnover. The lack of consistent occupancy led to neglect. The manor slowly but surely crept into disrepair. The bills mounted up, and the owners finally decided to get rid of it completely and put it up for sale.

Considering its condition and remote location, they were amazed that an American family fell in love with it online. Bill, Diane, and their daughter, Elena, flew over and placed an offer immediately after viewing it.

Their dream was to open a mindfulness and meditation-themed B & B, with a small gourmet vegan restaurant. They felt that with all the hunting and fishing that was currently the main draw of the area, something as refreshingly zen as they had planned would be an immediate success.

Where their logic and business plan came from, nobody knew. What the locals did know however, was that the idea was ill-advised at best.

They spent a small fortune on the manor, working tirelessly to revamp the old farm house and turn it into a place of peace, rest and harmony.

It took them over a year to complete, but only six months to go bust.

No one, it seemed, had any interest in partaking in their advertised peace and harmony. One reason may have been its ambient backdrop of shotgun blasts and animal carcasses being driven to be butchered. When the Deffors bought the place, they had no idea that the hills and glens that surrounded it were prime hunting areas.

They sold the place at a huge loss, and realised they had no choice but to return to Maryland.

When the Deffors decided to throw in the towel and return to Maryland, their daughter, Elena, realised that she had no wish whatsoever to go back to her previous life. In the year and a half she had spent in the Highlands, she had found a people and a place that somehow resonated deeply within her psyche. The Highlands made her feel physically and mentally strong as well as safe. It wasn't an easy life in the northern reaches of Scotland, however the benefits, Elena felt, far outweighed the grey skies and long winters.

*

Elena was raised just outside Annapolis in the tiny town of Deale, Maryland. It was a strange mix of rednecks, meth addicts and fabulously wealthy horse breeders. You could turn off a road filled with run-down trailer homes, and end up on a five-hundred-acre horse property.

As if that dichotomy wasn't strange enough, Deale was also home to some of the most beautiful boat marinas on the Chesapeake.

Somehow, the eclectic array of people managed to co-exist and even thrive.

Elena's parents owned and ran the local hardware store. As it was the only one for ten miles in any direction, they did quite well. They also very cleverly managed to capture a nice bit of the marine chandlering business.

They only got that business through complete serendipity.

One afternoon, their store got a last-minute order for some stainless steel, three-inch clip fasteners and they were short by about fourteen. Not wanting to let their customer down, Bill decided to swing by the marine chandler and see if it had some to top up his order. What he found truly amazed him.

One entire side of the store was filled with fancy boat clothes adorned with nautical symbols and such. Bill thought the stuff was pretentious as well as being astronomically expensive.

A cotton T-shirt that would sell anywhere else for about ten dollars was thirty-nine dollars there. All because it had a tiny sailboat logo printed on it.

The other side of the store was the real eye-opener. It was filled with marine hardware: screws, bolts, chain, rope, fasteners, tools, all things that his store sold in town. Yet a two-inch S hook, that he would sell for seventy-five cents, was five dollars in the marine mega store. He spent almost an hour looking at just about every item they stocked and realised that they had at least half of them at their store.

The difference was that they called themselves a hardware store. That changed the following day. Their store ceased trading as Deale Hardware and Paint, and rebranded as Deale Hardware, Paint and Marine Supplies.

That's all they had to do.

In a five-mile radius of Deale, there were, conservatively, ten thousand boats. Everything from ten-foot, metal fishers to sixty-foot luxury power boats. Every single one of them needed marine hardware. Whether it was nylon line, a snap fastener, chrome cleaner, you name it – every boat owner ended up needing something on a daily basis.

The only stocking change they had to make was to increase their inventory with more stainless steel and brass.

Listing these with a sixty percent mark-up still put them seventy-five percent cheaper than the chandler's.

In a conscious effort not to mess with the chandler's business too badly, they vowed to not branch out beyond what they were already selling. The mega store could keep its monopoly for clothes, tenders, canoes, kayaks, canvas, etc.

They would just skim a little of its hardware trade.

The plan worked like magic. Their summer revenue increased by a whopping forty percent.

Elena was not a particularly good student, but by ten years old, was a budding entrepreneur. She had three businesses out of season, and five during the summers.

She had two paper routes, mowed lawns, would do limited grocery shopping (there was only so much she could carry on her bike) and in the summer, she washed boats and did laundry for the marina clientele.

The Deffors were also the only vegans in town, possibly in all of St George County.

Diane had once tried a social experiment and made vegan chicken and mushroom pies using tempeh instead of chicken. She offered free slices to anyone who wanted to try it at the monthly farmers' market.

Not one single person took her up on the offer. She didn't care. She was a great cook and was developing a whole range of vegan meals that were impressing the hell out of her family.

By the time Elena turned eighteen, the hardware store was still doing a roaring trade, Diane had found a few shops in Annapolis that would stock her vegan entrées and Elena was running twelve mini businesses.

Things were good.

Then suddenly they weren't.

The town's only pharmacy went under, and in what seemed to be a ludicrously short time, a new tenant took over the lease and moved in.

Great Price Hardware had arrived in Deale. GPH was the nation's largest hardware chain. They were known for undercutting all local competition until they were economically forced to fold their tents and leave town.

Despite the threat, the entire Deffor family put on their Sunday best and went to the grand opening. They walked in with a positive outlook. How bad could it really be?

That night they decided that they could no longer compete in the Deale hardware business, especially against a chain megastore. GPH was selling at a margin at least forty percent below what they needed to break even.

The Deffors held a going-out-of-business sale that lasted ten days.

Because their store had a prime, main-street location, it sold quickly to a group that wanted to turn it into a small local supermarket.

As Elena's businesses and Diane's vegan meal sales together didn't add up to a liveable salary, they decided that it was a sign that they needed to try something radically different.

Diane's family had originally been raised in Scotland and she had spent her early teens living in the Highlands. She had been having a hankering to visit it again, and maybe even stay for an extended period.

They started looking online for business opportunities and after a few weeks of looking, stumbled across the Waylight B & B.

After a super quick exploratory visit, they fell in love with the place and made an offer on the spot.

*

When their vegan B & B scheme, and a good portion of their savings, disintegrated before their eyes, they decided that they had no choice but to return stateside, and try to find a way to recoup some of their money.

In an effort to start off on a cost-conscious path, they accepted the offer from Bill's parents to live with them.

It certainly wasn't the dream they had strived for, but at least they had some money from the B & B sale and were certain they could find a way to make things work. Just not in Scotland.

Elena, however, felt that Scotland was where she was meant to be. She managed to convince the new buyers to keep her on. Her pitch was that she knew the place inside and out, and could help them navigate the oddities of opening and running a hospitality business in the Highlands.

CHAPTER
TWO

The new buyers, Helen and Leon Frank, were Londoners with no hospitality experience. They knew very little about the Scottish Highlands and its ways, yet had a very specific idea of what they wanted the old manor farm to become.

Their concept for the Waylight was vastly different from their predecessors. They wanted to turn the place into a boutique hunting destination. It was to have a restaurant/bar serving locally hunted and butchered game, together with a decent array of single malts.

The bed and breakfast was cosmetically remodelled in under three months. The gentle earth tones were papered over and the vegan-friendly chairs and sofas were sold to a pub in Inverness. They were replaced with predominately heavy wood and leather furniture. Tartan wallpaper, Highland-themed fabrics and mounted animal heads rounded off the new design palette.

They renamed it The Lodge, though the locals continued to call it the Waylight B & B.

They opened on 22nd December with a special ten-night, all-inclusive Christmas and New Year holiday package. As part of their opening campaign, they focussed on the amazing hunting and challenging fishing, together with what they promised would be exquisite food and drink. The four guest rooms sold out surprisingly quickly.

*

Andrew wasn't feeling remotely zenish as he pulled up outside the old bed and breakfast. The first thing he noticed was that the Franks, in an effort to make the place look Christmassy, had draped twinkle lights on every tree and shrub they could find. They had also covered the house itself with enough full-sized, multicoloured Christmas lights to illuminate a small stadium.

The gaudy explosion of artificial illumination in the midst of miles and miles of black nothingness was highly disconcerting.

He reluctantly stepped out of the warm cocoon-like feel of the tiny car, and into the howling, freezing winds of a late December storm.

He could see from the increased size of the flakes that it was going to be exactly what the buggers at the weather bureau had predicted. A major snowstorm. At least it showed that they could get it right occasionally.

He looked at The Lodge and wondered why anyone would have bought the place. It wasn't attractive or welcoming. Built in the mid-nineteenth century, it had been constructed as a working manor farm. Practical, weatherproof and devoid of any frills or embellishments.

It was like a child's drawing of a house. It was a three-storey cube with a gabled roof and dormer windows sticking out of, what he presumed, was a converted loft. All the windows had heavy shuttering which was currently open. The entry was up a few steps from the gravel forecourt. The solid oak door looked to have been hewn from local timber. A small half-circle pane of glass was cut into the top third of the door.

The house was built with local stone, which may have once been a pale sandy grey, but had, over time, weathered to near black. The slate roof was so dark, it seemed to meld into the night sky.

From the outside, it looked anything but inviting. The wood plaque over the entrance, with the words 'THE LODGE' painted in red, did nothing to soften the tone.

Andrew took a moment to listen. All he could hear was the wind howling through the tall pines that surrounded the property and the window shutters that, though open and secured, were rattling against the house.

Between gusts, he heard nothing.

Andrew took note that there were a total of seven vehicles in front of the building. Two were recent reg BMWs, one Jag, one mid-sized Vauxhall (he guessed it to be a rental out of Inverness), one older Ford Fiesta, a classic but unrestored Mini, and a heavily worked Nissan pickup that probably belonged to the hotel.

Andrew checked his mobile though he knew it wouldn't have any signal. Not up there.

His screen showed two bars. He was astounded. Then, as he watched, the bar count went from two to one to zero, then the words 'no signal' appeared.

He sighed and put the phone into his inside coat pocket. He wasn't going to be using it, that was for sure.

He was just about to try the door handle when it swung open. Elena Deffor stood in the entryway. She looked like an artist's depiction of a Scottish warrior maiden. She was dressed in a dark green velvet suit, with a bright red blouse underneath. The outfit accentuated her flowing mane of vibrant red hair. She looked to be taller than Andrew, but it was hard to tell with her thick-soled Doc Martins.

"Hi, I'm Elena. I'm the one who tried to call you."

"I'm Constable Whiting. You're American!"

She smiled, creating dimples in her cheeks. "I know. Come in. It's freezing."

Inside, the twinkle light extravaganza continued. A Christmas tree that was way too big for the space dominated the entry hallway. It was heavily adorned with cheap, multicoloured baubles and strand after strand of coloured LED lights that blinked frantically from hue to hue. The result was frenetic and jarring. Also, anyone needing to pass through the area had to work their way cautiously around the green coniferous obstacle.

Despite the garish entrance, things calmed as they went deeper into the house.

Elena led Andrew into the formal dining room. Every effort had been made to make it look Scottish, from its tartan drapes and plaid woven wool carpeting to its thistle-embossed wallpaper. The chairs were dark wood with forest green leather cushioning. A gleaming mahogany dining table, dressed in holiday cheer, was the main focal point of the room.

The second focal point was the dead body splayed out on the green carpet near the room's only window.

The body was male, and looked to be in his fifties. He was lying on his back and was dressed festively. He wore a dark burgundy dinner jacket, emerald green trousers and an extraordinarily frilly mauve dress shirt. The outfit was capped off with a bright green and red striped bow tie. His face was blue-grey, darkening to purple at the back of his neck and head.

As Andrew tried to take in the bizarre tableau, Helen Frank entered the room. Though now in her forties, she looked ten years younger. Her complexion had that raw, healthy glow that comes from too much time outside in cold conditions.

"About time!" She glared at Andrew.

Andrew had no intention of starting things off with him getting a bollocking.

"If you've not noticed, there's a bugger of a storm out there and it would have taken me an hour to drive here, even in decent weather."

"I'll give you that," she conceded. "Sorry. Didn't mean to snap at you."

"Can you tell me what happened, Mrs…?"

"Frank. Helen Frank. My husband and I own The Lodge."

Before Helen could say any more, Elena interrupted.

"Can I get you both a cup of tea, or something stronger?"

"I'd love a tea, please." Andrew jumped right in. "Two sugars and a wee drop of milk."

Helen opted for a large brandy. Andrew had a feeling that it was far from her first of the night.

"We were all at the table having our dinner. We'd started with locally smoked trout. The main was roast quail. Alan – that's Alan – Mr Hutchings." She pointed at the body.

"We were all tucking in while telling stories about people's worst Christmases. Alan was halfway through a funny story about his mother managing to serve an undercooked turkey that practically killed his whole family, when he started to choke. At first we thought he was joking. Then as he started to turn blue we realised it was something serious. Leon got him to his feet and tried the Heimlich manoeuvre. It did force up a good-sized piece of spud, but he still couldn't breathe. I tried to reach into his throat with my fingers and felt a bone, presumably from the quail, stuck across his windpipe. We tried everything, but just couldn't get it out.

"We gave him CPR where you see him now. Must have been for over twenty minutes, but it didn't do any good. We would have covered him up, but my husband felt that you lot would probably not want us to disturb anything."

"Thank you, Mrs Frank. Your husband was right. Did you call for an ambulance?"

"Out here? You must be joking. The nearest A & E is in Inverness. Besides, the phone has been playing up since yesterday. The only time it's worked was when Elena managed to get through to you. It's dead again now."

"Was he here with anybody?"

"No. He was our only single guest. He loved hunting though; in fact, he was the one who shot the quail we were eating."

"And that ultimately killed him," Andrew added.

"What an odd thing to say. You're of course quite right – but still."

"I'll have to see if I can get a doctor up here tonight. He'll need to certify the death."

"Or she!" Elena said.

Andrew gave her a knowing glance. "Or she."

Helen smiled then had a thought. She looked troubled.

"Problem?" Andrew asked.

"I hate to sound uncaring, but we have six other paying guests in The Lodge who are expecting to be wined and dined for the next nine days. Does – Alan have to remain in here?"

"Have you checked with your other guests? Do they even plan to stay after this?"

"Yes. My husband did. They have nowhere else to go at this point. They've all come a long way. Besides, it wasn't as if anyone here actually knew him. He was just a paying guest."

"I will have to check with my governor about moving him."

"How do you intend to do that? Have you looked outside?"

Andrew looked puzzled. He was about to check the dining room window, but realised that doing so would require him to practically stand on the body. He walked out of the room, around the tree and out of the front door.

He was stunned at the vista before him. What had been about thirty centimetres of snow when he arrived at The Lodge, was now at least half a metre in places. He could only see as far as the Christmas lights illuminated, but that was enough. There was nothing but a blanket of white. There was no sign of the entry drive or the lane beyond. The falling flakes were the size of leaves.

If his police car had better clearance, he might have risked it, but the Fiesta simply wouldn't stand a chance in that much snow.

"Bugger," he mumbled to himself.

"Beautiful, isn't it?" Elena said.

"Sorry, miss, I didn't know you were there."

"Sorry for what? Swearing? That's the least of the world's problems. I've been known to string a few obscenities together myself. Anyway, your tea's ready in the kitchen."

"Where's that?"

Elena reached over and took his hand without a second thought. She actually led him through the hall and to a back passageway that opened into the kitchen.

It was, like all working farm kitchens, a big functional space. It was designed to be the central core of the house. Farm staff would have gathered there for their meals and to discuss any business at hand.

It had been recently modernised into a professional-looking chef's kitchen. The old wood stove had been replaced with a six-burner hob and triple oven. An American-style double-door fridge dominated one wall. Custom cabinetry took up almost all the other wall space.

Leon Frank was putting the final few pieces of cutlery into an industrial-sized dishwasher. He was a big burly man. Roughly the same age as Helen and with the same wind-blown complexion.

He turned and introduced himself to Andrew.

"Nice kitchen," Andrew commented.

"We have the Yanks to thank for that. It must have cost them a fortune. Can't really see the point. How much equipment does it take to cook vegetables?"

"You know that's not the case, Leon," Elena said.

"Sorry, Elena. Didn't see you come in."

"Yeah, right!"

The banter seemed to be a regular thing.

"Mr Frank, I was wondering if either you could drive me, or if not – you would let me drive your four-by-four into town. I could alert my super and find a doctor who might be willing to come out here today."

"I'd be happy to lend you the old bucket of bolts, but it doesn't seem to be running."

"Since when?"

"Sometime yesterday. I was going to do a quick run into town around noon but the little bugger wouldn't start."

"May I try?" Andrew asked.

"If you think you can do any better, then by all means." He opened a utility drawer and removed a set of keys. "Here you go."

Andrew took them and headed back towards the front door.

"You don't have to go that way around. Go out the service door." Leon pointed to a small alcove off the kitchen. A door led directly outside. He noticed another structure behind the main house.

"What's the building out back?"

"Part general shed, part dressing room and locker."

"You have a gym?" Andrew asked.

Leon couldn't help but laugh.

"No. Dressing as in dressing a carcass. And the locker's a meat locker. We hang our game to age it."

"I take it the Americans didn't build that?"

"Bloody right. I'm not sure that ageing particularly helps fruit and vegetables."

Andrew stepped out onto the frozen white blanket.

CHAPTER
THREE

The snow was deep enough to cover his shoes. He could feel the icy wetness as it melted down his ankles and soaked his feet.

He reached the pickup and was surprised at just how much snow had fallen. It was as high as the running board.

He climbed in, inserted the key and heard the engine turn over. He tried ten times. It turned over perfectly. It just wouldn't fire. Leon was right. The bugger wasn't going to start.

Andrew popped the bonnet and walked to the front of the vehicle. He had to use his coat to clear some snow from the top. He used his police-issue Maglite to see if there was anything blatantly amiss in the engine compartment.

The moment he leaned over the engine, he could smell the overpowering stench of diesel fuel. He had to step onto the front bumper to get a vantage point into the engine compartment. Thankfully, it was an older model, so all the important bits were visible and recognisable.

He couldn't quite see the area around the fuel pump because someone had left a black cloth wrapped around the various hoses. He tried to grab the end of it.

It turned around, hissed angrily, then tried to bite his hand. It wasn't a cloth. It was a large black Highland rat.

Andrew was so shocked, he jumped backwards off the bumper and landed flat on his back in a growing snowdrift.

"Oh no you don't," he fumed.

He got back up and removed his expanding police-issue baton. He extended it with one flick then got back on the bumper. The rat was still there. It was glaring back at him, seemingly protective of the fuel pump. Andrew prodded the rodent with the baton end, which only angered it further.

He had to go to option two. He removed the pepper spray canister from his belt, slid the safety cap to the side, and sprayed a good stream of the stuff directly into the rat's eyes.

It went mad.

Andrew decided to give the little beast some room, and backed away from the truck. He heard a great deal of commotion in the engine compartment, then witnessed something that was guaranteed to give him nightmares for years.

A black sea of rats came pouring out of the engine compartment both from the top and from the undercarriage. They flowed out of the Nissan and scurried away from it as fast as they could. Once clear of the pepper spray effect however, they quickly regrouped and turned towards Andrew.

The largest rat – the one he'd sprayed – seemed to be leading the pack directly towards him. Their black colony stood out against the fresh white snow.

He tried to back up, but tripped and fell arse first into the same snowdrift.

They continued to stalk him. Slowly. Cautiously. Countless pairs of red eyes stared directly at him. Their little mouths opened and closed as they hissed at him. Their yellow teeth seemed to reflect the light from the Christmas illuminations.

He tried to move his feet away from the approaching mass, but his shoes kept slipping on the icy surface.

The lead rat crept towards Andrew's feet. The others followed closely behind. It stopped and sniffed at Andrew's black police shoes. It then started to climb on one of them. Andrew shook his foot as hard as he could but the rat held on tight.

A few other rats followed their alpha and scurried onto his shoes. Others started to make their way up his legs. Andrew tried to find the pepper spray but realised he had dropped it when he fell backwards. The cannister now sat in the centre of the rat pool.

Andrew felt a scream working its way up from his gut.

"Oh, for heaven's sake. Shoo!" Elena stepped between Andrew and the rodent attack squad. She swept them aside with a broom. She also gently brushed off the ones on his feet and legs. Silently, they scattered and vanished into the night.

Andrew watched in complete horror (and relief) as the last few darted into the darkness.

"They're not dangerous. All the farms up here are riddled with them. You just have to be firm."

She gave him a hand to get up from the soft snow.

"Thank you," Andrew said.

"Are you okay? You look a little frazzled."

"Me? No! That sort of thing happens all the time."

He tried to compose himself as he walked back to the pickup and shone his torch at the fuel pump.

"That could be the problem."

"Let me see." Elena pushed up next to him and looked. He could feel her warmth next to him.

He tapped the diesel fuel pump. "See this thingy here?"

"Yeah. I see it."

"Well, look at the rubber hoses attached to it."

"Are they supposed to be chewed up like that?" Elena asked.

"No, they are not. Your furry friends have managed to gnaw their way through all the fuel hoses."

"Is that normal?"

"Sometimes a single rat or even mouse might decide to chew a hose to make more room for a nest, but not that many!" Andrew answered.

"So, no driving into town then?"

He couldn't be sure but it almost sounded like she was teasing him.

On the way back to the side door, Andrew checked his mobile, just in case.

No service.

"Let's try your landline, in case that's working now," Andrew suggested.

"I'm not sure there's much point."

"There's always a point. You just never know."

Elena took his hand (again) and led him past the service door to the far corner of the shed. She pointed to the utility pole a few feet away.

He used his torch to light up the pole. He could just make out the top through the heavy snow and darkness. A black cable, that seemed to appear magically from the endless gloom, was attached to a metal junction box. The cable that should have led to the lodge was hanging loose. There seemed to be only a few feet of it left, and that was whipping madly in the freezing gale.

"Please tell me that isn't the phone line," Andrew asked.

"Okay. That's not the phone line."

"You're messing with me, aren't you?"

"Just a little."

"So that is the phone line?" Andrew asked.

"Yes, sir."

"What about internet?"

She pointed to the dancing cable. "It used the phone line."

Andrew stared up at the cable for a moment.

"Let's go back inside then. Oh, and Elena—"

"Yes?"

"There's no need to call me sir."

She smiled to herself as they plodded back through the deepening snow.

*

Helen and Leon were standing in the kitchen watching the snow accumulate behind the house. The kitchen light cast enough illumination to see the huge flakes whipping by almost horizontally.

Leon took Helen's hand and turned to her.

"Things will be fine."

"You sure? This wasn't quite what we planned for the opening."

Leon kissed the tip of her nose. "You know I've always found a way to make things work."

"Yes, you have."

"Then don't doubt me now. Don't let this one incident spoil everything."

Helen grabbed his hand, squeezed it tightly then kissed it. She knew he was right. She also knew that he'd do whatever it took to make The Lodge a success.

*

Helen was originally from Yorkshire and was raised on a large working farm. As a child, she helped out (she had little choice) with the myriad of tasks that exist on a rural working property. She initially was kept away from the nastier jobs, but as she got older, all that changed. Like all independent UK farms, subsidies and competition from the factory farms had, over the years, eroded their profits.

The few full-time farm hands were let go and they had to depend on part-time help. Soon, even they became a luxury, and the family was forced to rely on their own blood and sweat to keep the farm going.

At the young age of thirteen, Helen had to start taking part in the animal slaughtering. Usually for food processing, but occasionally when a livestock disease necessitated the massacring of animals within entire counties.

That was the hardest part. Just because there was a suspected case of some bovine or porcine illness on a farm thirty miles away, they were required by law to slaughter their herds. Their once strong and valuable animals ended up dead and piled high in the middle of their grazing field. They were then burned in one giant death pyre.

Though she hated it, she became very used to animal slaughter.

The same year Helen turned sixteen, the farm went under. Her parents sold the property and, in a bizarre and unexpected move, bought a townhouse in the hills behind Mijas in the south of Spain.

Helen had no urge to go with them. She had no friends in Spain, didn't speak a word of Spanish, and was in the middle of studying for her A levels.

She was given no choice. They packed up the few belongings they felt they might need in Spain, and gave the rest to charity. Helen was in tears the day they drove away from their old farm. It was the only home she'd ever known and couldn't even imagine starting over in a foreign country.

They drove to Folkestone where they caught the channel car ferry. She'd never been on a boat, let alone one where you drive right into its middle. The trip across to France took almost three hours because of the stormy seas. All three of them got seasick within minutes after leaving the Folkstone breakwater.

They weren't alone. Just about everyone on board got seasick at some point on the journey. Some poor sods were throwing up for the entire three hours.

Finally, nauseous, pale and slightly disorientated, they drove off the ferry at the sea terminal just outside the city of Boulogne. They managed to drive as far as Tours on that first day. They thought about driving through and taking turns at the wheel, but for their first night outside England, they chose to stay in a budget motel just off the autoroute.

The rest of the trip took three days, during which they only stopped at a motel for one night. The car became claustrophobic. They felt dirty and short-tempered. Their mood greatly improved when they finally joined the coast road at Valencia in the south of Spain.

Helen stared out of the car window at the whitewashed buildings, the seaside towns with their ocean-front tavernas and restaurants, and the glorious Mediterranean.

They stopped and ate the local fish stew – Suquet de Peix. It was delicious. Helen had never tasted anything so exotic in her life. When they ate fish in England it was in a thick crunchy batter served alongside thick-cut chips.

The most exciting moment was when they reached the city of Malaga and turned inland. They were almost home.

When they pulled up to their townhouse, Helen was amazed. It was bigger than their farmhouse. It was three storeys tall with a roof terrace offering a view all the way to the coast. Their fears of making a home in Spain diminished a bit as they explored the property.

That night, too tired to cook, they walked into the picturesque village of Mijas. They ate outside on a brick terrace that faced olive-tree-covered hills that sloped down to the city of Fuengirola. Beyond that, they could just make out the top of the rock of Gibraltar, some hundred kilometres away.

The food was simple but fresh and delicious. They all had a glass of the local Rioja wine, Helen included.

They felt a strange sense of contentment as they walked back to their townhouse.

The next challenge for Helen was starting school. It was one hundred percent Spanish-speaking and the curriculum *was not A level based at all. The local children her age were studying for their Titulo de Bachillerato.*

The first day was terrifying. The other students looked at her as if she was some new creature they'd never seen before. A few tried to talk with her, but they spoke only Spanish and she didn't know a single word in their language.

She was miserable for the first few months, and became withdrawn and despondent. Then something magical happened. Without knowing it, she found she'd picked up enough Spanish to actually converse with her peers.

She started to actually enjoy Spain. She loved the school trips to places like Alhambra and Granada and began to relish her new life in a foreign country.

She also started to like Spanish boys. They were so much more mature that their British counterparts. They were also far more experienced at romance and, even at sixteen, the art of seduction.

One such boy lived in a townhouse, two doors down from hers. Miguel was tall, had an athlete's body and dark eyes that, when focussed on her, sent a gentle shiver the whole way down her spine.

They started dating casually, which is pretty much all you can do at that age in a predominantly Catholic country. They kissed and tried a little extracurricular exploring, but that's where it ended.

They had to use Helen's room to 'study'. Miguel's father refused to let them be alone in his house. He still believed that couples should be chaperoned right up until their wedding day.

Helen's parents couldn't have cared less. They knew perfectly well what was going on upstairs but trusted their daughter to keep the fondling above the waist.

Helen knew that she was falling in love with Miguel. She hadn't told him, and he had said nothing along those lines to her. She decided that the next time they were together, she would let him know.

That day came the following week. They had been kissing on the bed for almost thirty minutes straight. Helen decided that the time was right.

Fate had other plans.

Her mother knocked on the door then without even waiting for an answer walked in. She asked Miguel to leave as they needed to talk to their daughter urgently.

After Miguel reluctantly left, Helen joined her parents at the dining table. They both looked very serious.

Her father had just come back from the doctor's office. It seemed that his thirty years of two packs a day smoking had caught up with him.

His recent weight loss and night coughing bouts were not allergy-related as he had hoped. He had lung cancer.

They had not been residents long enough for all their benefit eligibilities to kick in, so any treatment would be at their cost. Six months later and it would have been free.

Their only option was to return to the UK and the waiting arms of the NHS.

Helen couldn't believe what they were telling her. They had ripped her from her life and friends in England just six months earlier. Now that she was actually integrating into the Spanish life, they were going to do it again. This time in reverse. What was worse was that they weren't even going back to Yorkshire, which she at least knew. No, they were going to have to live in London because of the better access to cancer specialists and treatment centres.

In the end, she knew she had no choice. Her father was ill. He could even die. Of course, they had to go back.

She cried for two days straight. She wept in Miguel's arms. Despite Helen's pleas, one week later they flew back into Gatwick in the midst of a heavy grey downpour. They couldn't waste time on the long drive through Spain and France. They needed to get him back in England and under treatment immediately.

They moved into a rented flat, just off Broughton Road in Fulham. Her father began radiation and chemotherapy treatments within a matter of days.

Helen started at the London Oratory School two days after landing so she could get back on track for her A levels.

She was miserable. She again had no friends, and found herself in strange, unfamiliar surroundings.

After a few weeks the doctor advised her father that he was responding to the radiation. Despite the good news, he remained sullen and bad-tempered.

Meanwhile, her mother had discovered Cinzano and was drowning her misery in sickly sweet vermouth.

Life really was the pits!

Then, on a bleak Tuesday while trying to force down the school's unseasoned and overcooked lunch offering, Leon Frank sat down across from her.

"So, you're the new bird from Spain?"

That had made her laugh.

CHAPTER
FOUR

Andrew found both Helen and Leon in the kitchen.

"I've decided that we will have to do something with the body. I have no idea how long we'll be stuck up here. It would be best if we could place him somewhere that won't expedite decomposition any further. Tell me more about the dressing and locker rooms. We shouldn't freeze him – that will make the doctor's job twice as difficult."

"Neither room is below freezing, but the dressing room would probably be best," Leon suggested. "It's refrigerated, but only to four degrees, so he definitely won't freeze, plus there's no meat currently there. I'd prefer a dead body not to go into the hanging locker with our week's food."

"That sounds like a plan. Is there somewhere in the dressing room we could lay the body, other than on the floor?"

"There's a long butcher's table. It's clean and plenty big enough."

"Perfect. Last thing – we're going to need to physically get him out there."

Leon suddenly looked concerned. "I can't ask my guests to help carry a corpse. Can you imagine what that could do to our Yelp ratings?"

Andrew was at a loss for words.

"I think the four of us could manage him," Elena offered. "Each one takes a limb!"

"Good heavens!" Helen said. "I don't know if I could!"

"I've seen you swing a 40-kilo roebuck over your shoulder and carry it all the way to the pickup!" Leon reminded her.

"I planned on eating the buck."

"I don't see the difference," Leon replied.

"Alan was a guest!"

"Even more reason to get him out of the house with some degree of dignity. With four, we can carry him without having to drag him through the snow and muck."

"Christ! All right then. I'll help."

"Would it be okay for me to clear the dinner things from the table?" Elena asked. "We left everything exactly as it was when…"

"I don't see why not. Can it wait till we move the body?" Andrew asked.

"Sure!" Elena seemed pleased with the answer.

*

Alan's journey to the outbuilding was relatively uneventful, despite his weighing far more than any of them had imagined. They were definitely going to feel it in their backs the next day.

Once positioned on the butcher's table, Helen returned to The Lodge and retrieved a green plaid sheet from the linen cupboard. They all took a corner and were about to drape it over his body.

"Where's his bow tie gone?" Andrew asked.

"Probably outside somewhere," Leon said. "Does it matter?"

"I guess not. Doubtful it played much of a part in the incident."

They laid the sheet carefully over Alan's corpse.

"Should we say something?" Elena asked.

Helen seemed impatient to get back into The Lodge. "Like what?"

"I know!" Leon said. "Thanks for the quail! They were delicious."

Helen shook her head as she stepped out of the dressing room. "You really are a pig sometimes!"

Leon headed after her, realising that he may have underdone the eulogy.

*

Leon Frank had been born in London's East End, just a stone's throw from Stepney Green. His father had a fruit stall at Berwick Street Market in Soho. The stall had been handed down to him from his father and his father before that.

It wasn't an easy life. He'd be at the fruit and veg wholesalers at 4 a.m. bidding for the day's fresh merchandise. He'd then have to get it to the market stall before 7 a.m. so he could get his clapped-out van parked before the rush hour began. He'd then display the produce carefully, hiding the spoiled stuff under the fresher pieces.

By eight, the market would be in full swing. He'd man his stall until 7 p.m. then have to sort what to keep, and what to sell off for pennies on the pound to the local punters.

He'd stagger home, exhausted and hungry. He'd have a quick wash, drink a few cans of Stella with his supper, then pass out on the sofa.

That was life in the Frank house six days a week. Leon's mum kept the house tidy and comfortable, while at the same time worked four days a week at the laundromat five streets away. Her eight-hour days there were spent doing other people's laundry and dry-cleaning.

Leon, even by the age of six, knew that he didn't want to have to work like his parents when he grew up. He had no idea what he would do, but fruit, veg and laundry just weren't going to be in his future.

Unfortunately for Leon, his father didn't care what Leon wanted out of life. He was a Frank and the Franks had been working the markets for over two hundred years. Leon was going to have the stall after his father retired and that was that.

His mother knew that Leon was going to have a tough go of it. She hoped he'd find his way somehow, but knew that her husband was already planning his future in the market.

His father took him out of school at fourteen and started bringing him to work every day. Training, he called it. He would tell stories of how he and his father, Leon's grandad, would work in blizzards, gales, heatwaves, whatever. 'You can't just close your stall because of a few drops of rain. People depend on you,' he'd say.

The more his father tried to sell him on the idea, the more determined Leon became to get away from the East End and Berwick Street. He had no intention of spending his life standing around all day hoping to sell some 'luverly sprouts'.

His escape plan started to materialise when he turned seventeen. A schoolfriend's father had decided, after long consideration, to take on a paid apprentice to help him with his plastering business.

Leon secretly met with him and the two got on well. They shook hands after less than thirty minutes. Leon had found a possible way out of the fruit and veg game.

When Leon told his father about his apprenticeship, he hoped the old man might have actually been proud of him. Instead, he threatened to throw him out of the house and cut him out of their lives forever.

His dad had never been a deep-thinking and rational human being.

His mum informed his father that if he threw Leon out, she'd be off as well, and he could take care of the bloody house by himself. He stormed out, had a skinful with his mates, slept in the van, then joined his wife and son for breakfast the next morning.

He agreed to let Leon give it a go.

Leon's new boss, Peter Willow, had made one strict condition. Leon was to go back and finish school. He would let him work evenings and weekends, but until he had at least a few A levels under his belt, he wasn't going to bring him on full-time. He couldn't stress highly enough how important a few educated thoughts could be in one's life.

The pay was good. The work was hard but rewarding. It turned out Leon had quite an artistic flair. Within two years

Peter called him aside one day and told him that he honestly believed he was one of the best plasterers he'd ever worked with. His attention to detail and sense of dedication to the craft were stellar.

In the run up to his A levels, he was having to learn the different styles of plastering at the same time as being buried in books about history and economics.

Despite the hard graft and long days, he was finally happy about the direction his life was going. He just wanted the exams to be over and for him to be able to work full-time.

His economics teacher took him aside one day and suggested that he attend a special one-day cramming class at a school in Fulham. The person giving the class was apparently some sort of economics guru. His teacher felt the one-day session might help him get through the A level.

Reluctantly, Leon took the tube to Parson's Green Station at some godawful time of the morning, and walked the rest of the way to some dump called the London Oratory School.

The all-day class was intense. Leon had never tried to cram so much data into his head in such a short period of time. At the morning break he met some local lads who actually attended the school. They swapped stories about which school had the worst food, the cutest birds and the shittiest teachers. After the thirty-minute break he returned to the classroom and prepared himself mentally for the next hundred and sixty minutes of economics.

By lunchtime, he had a blazing headache.

He walked into the cafeteria and piled his tray with what looked to be pretty decent nosh, then looked for a place to sit. He saw this one girl sitting alone. She sounded like one *of the ones his new mates had mentioned.*

He decided it was her lucky day. He sat across from her, took one look at her hazel eyes and felt his entire world wobble on its axis.

CHAPTER
FIVE

"Can I offer you a change of clothes, Constable?" Leon offered once they were back inside. "You might as well be comfortable while you wait."

"Thank you, but I'm not supposed to be out of uniform while on duty."

"I think it's fair to say that you don't have to be on duty again until we can either drive out, or someone from your lot turns up here. I'll tell you what, why don't you use Alan's room then you could have a sleep and a nice shower in the morning?"

Andrew gave him a concerned look.

Leon got the drift immediately. "Alan arrived today and only spent a few minutes in the room. It's never been slept in."

Andrew felt relieved. It would be nice to have somewhere to put his head down. "Obviously if the situation changes—"

"Understood," Leon said.

"Where were you planning to spend your Christmas before you got stuck with us?" Elena asked.

"Actually, I was going to go and catch up on some laundry and cleaning, then check out the pub. See what they had planned for Christmas dinner."

"You weren't going to spend it with friends or family?" Helen said.

"My parents died ten years ago. I haven't actually made too many friends up here yet, so it's just me."

"How did they die?" Elena asked.

"Head on collision on the A1(M). A lorry managed to go down the wrong way on the off-ramp. Strangely, that's what got me to join the force."

That put an end to any additional conversation.

"Well, you'll just have to suffer and spend Christmas with us," Helen said.

"I expect to be able to leave by then, but thank you very much for the offer."

"I think you're being a little optimistic. This storm looks like it's going to be with us at least through Christmas." Leon put his hand on Andrew's shoulder. "It's gone eleven. We should all get a few winks before morning. Elena, will you show the constable upstairs?"

"I think you can start calling me Andrew, don't you?"

"Elena, would you please show Andrew to room four?"

"Sure. Do you need anything from your car?" Elena asked.

"Ta, but no." He gestured to himself. "This is all I've got!"

Leon gave him a sympathetic smile. "I'll put some things outside your door."

"Come on then." Elena grabbed his hand and led him out of the kitchen.

The trip to the room was the first time he was able to get a look at some of the other areas of The Lodge. They passed a comfortable-looking lounge. The door was open a few inches but he could clearly see a massive fireplace dominating one wall. A fire was burning in the grate as a few guests, drinks in hand, were relaxing before going to bed.

Andrew decided that the following morning was probably the best time to introduce himself to the other guests. His chance of getting sober answers from them was much more likely after breakfast than after dinner.

Next to the lounge was a small but inviting bar. Backlit glass shelving showed off their decent selection of single malts.

Elena noticed his glance at the bottles, and the involuntary licking of his lips.

"Wait here," she instructed.

She ran into the bar, went behind the counter and poured him a triple measure of Aberlour. She handed him the glass.

"Something to sip in your room before you sleep. It'll help you relax."

They headed upstairs and down a hallway that ran the length of The Lodge. There were three doors on either side. Number four was the second on the right.

"Which is your room?" Andrew asked.

"Don't get any funny ideas, Constable."

"I wasn't – I was just—"

"I'm teasing. My room is on the floor above. My parents converted the entire loft. That's where the Franks live as well. It's very comfy."

Elena opened the door with a pass key. Thankfully, Alan had been a very tidy man. The room was immaculate.

"I'll remove all of his things tomorrow if that's all right?"

"You don't need to bother. I'll find a place for them."

"No one's slept in the bed yet. You'll be the first," Elena announced.

"I'll just lie on top."

"Don't be silly. Get under the covers and have a real sleep. You may need your wits about you tomorrow."

He gave her a puzzled look.

"It's Christmas Eve!"

She stepped into him and kissed him once, gently on the cheek, then turned and walked away. Andrew watched her go. He hoped she'd look back.

She didn't.

He had a quick poke around the room and the ensuite. He was delighted to see that there was a generous collection of courtesy items, including a couple of toothbrushes, toothpaste, even a brush and comb. All were wrapped and sealed in sanitary plastic. He was also glad to see that Alan didn't appear to have used any of the towels either, so maybe he would take a shower in the morning.

He sat on the end of the bed and drank half his Scotch. "Bloody hell! That's lovely."

He downed the rest, removed his shoes, then lay back on the bed with the intention of going back over the past day. He was asleep within seconds.

He dreamed of rats wearing blue bow ties.

*

He could easily have slept through the entire day if it weren't for the smell of freshly brewed coffee. It grabbed his senses like one of the old classic cartoons, where the smell grabs hold of your nose and pulls you along in a trance.

There was no actual nose pulling, but the smell and his rumbling stomach reminded him that he hadn't eaten a thing in almost twenty-four hours.

He took a quick shower, donned a pair of jeans and a cable knit sweater from the collection Leon had left at his door, then descended in search of sustenance.

He was not alone. The other guests were already in the dining room. They were moving along the breakfast buffet, plates at the ready. They hungrily perused the extraordinary display of morning goodies – sausages, bacon, eggs, pancakes, grilled tomatoes, mushrooms, even kippers!

It was a lot of food for six guests. Then again, they were probably paying a substantial amount for the ten-day package.

Andrew decided not to interrupt their time at the trough and to introduce himself after they'd eaten. Instead, he stuck his head in the kitchen and saw that Leon, Helen and Elena were busy finishing off the breakfast service, and starting to prep for the next meal.

"Morning all."

Leon actually seemed pleased to see him. "Andrew! So, how'd you sleep?"

"I haven't slept so well in years."

"Well, you obviously needed it!" Helen added.

"Would you like some breakfast?" Elena offered.

"I'd prefer not to interrupt the guests quite yet."

"You can eat in here. What would you like? I can get it for you."

"Those pancakes looked good!"

"American way?"

"What's that?"

Elena smiled proudly. "Masses of butter and maple syrup!"

"What have I got to lose? I'll give it a go. A coffee would go down a treat as well, if that's not too much trouble."

Elena gave him a playful punch on the arm and headed off to the dining room.

"That's a rather expansive breakfast selection you give your guests."

"They paid an expansive price," Leon replied.

"They can't possibly eat all that, can they?"

"God, I hope not," Helen laughed. "We freeze all the leftovers from the buffet. They end up in sausages, pasties and even, when I can be bothered, pâté."

"Have you looked outside yet?" Leon asked.

"Bugger! No. I completely forgot."

He looked to the kitchen window.

"Why're the shutters closed?"

"They're not!" Helen replied.

Andrew walked over to the window. His mind couldn't quite take in what he was looking at. The window was completely white, as if someone had painted it from the outside.

"That's not snow, is it?"

"It's certainly not fairy dust!" Leon joked. "It's not as bad as it looks. It's drifted against the back of the house.

Have a peek out the front. That'll give you a better idea."

Andrew walked by the oversized tree in the hall then opened the front door.

He gasped. Leon had been right. The back of the house was worse. The front however, came a close second. The overnight storm had laid a good metre more of snow onto the Highlands.

Only the roof of the pickup was visible in the courtyard. Where his police car was parked, there was now just a bump. The worst part was that it was still snowing. The flakes were a little smaller, but still – it didn't look like it had any intention of stopping any time soon.

Andrew realised that he wasn't going anywhere for the foreseeable future.

As he passed the hallway Christmas tree, he could swear it had got bigger. Not a lot, but a bit. It was getting harder to shimmy past the sturdy lower section.

He was almost past it, when a branch that he'd bent aside so he could pass, flipped back in place, burying a dozen pine needles into his hand.

"Bugger!" Andrew jumped clear of the tree and looked down.

The top of his hand was bleeding in twelve places. Not profusely by any means, but it was still blood. Plus, the punctured areas had started to itch.

"Brilliant!"

He reached the kitchen just as Elena arrived with his pancakes and coffee. She noticed his hand.

"What happened?"

"The tree attacked me."

Helen and Leon both stopped what they were doing

and revealed their hands and arms. Apparently the tree was becoming a complete hazard to everybody.

"When I get a moment, I'm going to cut it back a little. Probably should have done that in the first place," Leon admitted.

Helen just rolled her eyes. "You think so?"

Elena placed Andrew's breakfast, plus a jug of maple syrup, on the oversized kitchen table.

"Eat while there's still room in here. Lunch prep is about to start. By the way, I didn't know if you wanted any bacon or sausage?"

"This is fine, thank you."

He looked a little perplexed about the syrup.

Elena stepped over, spread a large pat of butter over the top pancake, then poured a sizeable amount of syrup over the entire stack.

"Try it!"

"This looks more like pudding!"

"Try it!"

He reluctantly cut into the stack and forked a butter-laden, syrupy wedge, into his mouth.

Andrew's expression changed from concern to ecstasy. "Oh heavens! That's bloody delicious!"

"Don't talk with your mouth full," Elena grinned.

*

He was halfway through the stack when a woman screamed from the dining room.

"Now what?" Helen sighed.

The four ran into the room to find one of the guests, an

overly made-up woman in her late thirties, having her left hand wrapped in linen napkins. Blood was oozing from a nasty-looking cut.

"What happened?" Andrew's training kicked in. He marched straight over to her and examined the wound.

"I was just cutting a sausage with that damn knife and somehow cut my hand."

Andrew looked at the stag-handled knife lying askew by the side of her plate. There was no trace of blood that he could see on the blade, but the woman's breakfast plate looked like a war zone.

Blood had splattered over it and partially melded with her scrambled eggs. Her two sausages both had blood on one end, giving them the appearance of severed fingers. She had even managed to get blood into her glass of orange juice. It now resembled a tequila sunrise.

Andrew looked to Leon. "Do you have a first aid kit?"

Leon nodded and ran out of the room.

Andrew kept pressure on the cut as he clenched the now bloody napkin.

Leon returned quickly and opened a professional-sized first aid bag. Andrew was about to try out his recently learned triage skills, but Leon seemed to know exactly what he was doing.

He cleaned the wound, applied antiseptic cream, butterfly plasters, gauze pads, then bandaged the whole lot. Andrew hadn't seen better work at a hospital.

Andrew decided he may as well take advantage of the group gathering. He cleared his throat to get everyone's attention then introduced himself to the other guests.

The injured woman, Cynthia Adams, suggested he

use his given powers to arrest the entire cutlery set. She seemed to be taking the whole thing quite well. Of course, the massive brandy and pair of white pills Helen had dispensed before Leon's triage may have helped.

"This is my husband, Douglas." Cynthia gestured to her right.

"Like the writer?" Andrew blurted out.

"Haven't heard of him. Would I know his works?" Douglas couldn't have sounded more pompous had he tried. Andrew guessed old money and possibly a little inbreeding. The Savile Row shirt, gold cufflinks, and old-school tie may have been the clue.

"*Hitchhiker's Guide*?" Andrew suggested.

"I don't read guidebooks. I prefer French literature of the nineteenth century."

Andrew managed to suppress a laugh. An older man across the table did not. He did more than laugh. He brayed.

"Sorry. Don't know what came over me. I'm Harry Stone and on my left, is my better half, Anne."

"Nice to meet you both." Andrew couldn't help but notice that Douglas Adams was glaring at Harry Stone. There was clearly some bad blood between the two.

The final pair both looked back at him with minimal interest, then returned their focus to their breakfast.

Thankfully, Leon stepped in. "Hilda and Walter Carter. They're up from London and happen to be our secret partners in The Lodge."

"I was called here last night because of the accidental death of a guest here at The Lodge," Andrew began. "Am I correct in assuming that all of you were present and were witness to the event?"

All either nodded or voiced their affirmative responses.

"Normally, a doctor would have been here by now and the cause of death could have been, if not confirmed, certainly theorised. Unfortunately, because of the storm, you're stuck with me.

"As the incident has yet to be ruled an accident, I am going to ask each of you, one at a time, to tell me what you saw yesterday evening. It won't take more than five minutes per person, and may expedite the process once others arrive.

"Leon, is there a small room I can use to not be under foot?"

"There's the morning room. It's tiny, but it'll do for what you need. Elena, would you show him where that is, please?"

Andrew faced the group before leaving. "I know this is not how you expected to spend Christmas Eve, but I promise this will be very quick. Let's start on my right. That means you, Mrs Adams, if you don't mind. When she comes back, would the next person on the right please join me?"

Cynthia stood up a little unsteadily. "You don't need to bother, Elena. I know the way."

Cynthia led Andrew around the hallway tree, to a small door immediately off the entry. She walked in and turned on the room's only light. A brass floor lamp with an animal-hide shade.

The room was indeed tiny. There was barely enough room for the two large leather armchairs and a tiny glass-topped table. It took Andrew a moment to realise that the table base was an elephant foot.

Cynthia sat in one of the chairs, cradling her wounded hand.

"Does it still hurt?" Andrew asked as he plopped down in the other chair.

"Actually, the brandy and the codeine have done wonders."

"Awful way to start your morning, an accident like that."

"It wasn't an accident!"

"But you said…"

"I know what I said. I didn't want to start a kerfuffle. But trust me. It wasn't an accident."

"If someone did that to you, you need to tell me – right now."

Cynthia took a long, slow breath, staring at Andrew the whole time. "Nobody did it to me. I was trying to cut the blasted sausage when I felt the knife pull to my left and then cut my left hand."

"You're saying the knife guided itself to your other hand?"

Cynthia gave him a glare that needed no translation. He decided to change direction. After all, brandy and codeine on an empty stomach…

"Let's hear about last night and what happened."

*

Andrew finished hearing the guests' versions within forty-five minutes. They were all pretty much the same. A few differed as to the details of the story Alan had been telling, but otherwise they matched. He only had one remaining witness.

Elena walked in and sat across from him.

"Thank you for your time, Elena."

"No problem. Did you know that you have beautiful eyelashes? They're so long." She leant forward to get a better look.

Andrew had to slide his chair back to stay a professional distance from her. "Sorry. This is a formal interview."

Elena smiled. "It's a bit late for formalities, don't you think? We kissed last night, after all."

Andrew could feel a blush rising to his cheeks. "We most certainly did not. You kissed my cheek. That was it."

"I don't remember you trying to stop me," Elena teased.

"I wasn't expecting it," Andrew insisted.

"So, you didn't like it?"

"That's not what I said. It just – bugger! Would you please let me interview you?"

"Of course, Constable." She feigned a serious expression but her eyes suggested something else as they held his.

"So, Miss—, I don't know your last name."

"Deffor."

"So, Miss Deffor, did you witness the incident that occurred last night in the dining room?"

"Yes. I was serving the vegetables when Alan started… do you need Alan's last name?"

"No. I have that already," Andrew replied.

"Anyway, I was serving vegetables when Alan suddenly started to cough. He drank some water but couldn't seem to breathe. He started choking. Leon – Mr Frank – gave him the Heimlich thing and he did cough up a piece of potato, but the choking got worse. Helen got him onto the floor and put her hand into his mouth. I'd never seen anyone do that before. It was kinda gross. Sorry – she said she could feel a bone stuck in his throat. She tried to get it out but couldn't. By that time, Alan's face was blue. Leon started performing CPR on him. They did it for ages but we could all see that he was gone."

"In your opinion then, it was an accident?"

"Yes – but there was one weird thing."

Andrew leaned towards her. "What was that?"

"After he'd died, everyone left the dining room. Leon had them go to the lounge. We left the dinner stuff undisturbed on the table in case the police needed to see it. Of course, it's all gone now. You remember you gave me permission to clear it all away?"

Andrew didn't like where the conversation was heading. "What was the weird thing?"

"I happened to look at Alan's plate. He'd eaten some of his veggies, but hadn't started on the quail yet."

Andrew gave her a puzzled look.

She rolled her eyes. She repeated it again, but slower.

"He ate his veggies but hadn't started on the quail yet."

Andrew still hadn't made the connection.

"He choked on a bone, didn't he?" she added.

"Oh bugger," Andrew said, finally catching on to Elena's concern.

"Where did the bone come from?"

*

Andrew stayed in the room for an additional half hour while he reviewed his notes and made a few observations of his own. He was relatively certain it was an accidental death, but the bone thing was odd. Where had it come from if it wasn't from his plate?

CHAPTER
SIX

Andrew returned to the dining room and found it empty. He checked the kitchen. Same thing. He then heard the sound of a hoover coming from the other side of the house. He followed the sound to the lounge where Elena was giving the room a quick clean.

It was the first time he had been fully inside the room. He wasn't surprised to see a continuation of the Scottish hunting theme with the usual tartans, rich leather and thistle-patterned drapes. In addition, there were two massive mounted stag heads, one above the fireplace, the other on the opposite wall. On the floor directly in front of the fireplace was a zebra-skin rug made from the entire animal. What really surprised him was the chandelier hanging from the centre of the ceiling.

It was at least two metres wide and made entirely from antlers. There were dozens of sharp-looking forks. Each had been drilled somehow, in order to wire tiny LED lights to the end of each point.

"Where is everyone?" He shuddered involuntarily.

Elena couldn't hear Andrew over the sound of the hoover and switched it off.

He asked again. This time she jumped. She hadn't been aware of him at all.

"The guests are back in their rooms, doing whatever you do after breakfast. Helen and Leon are in the outbuilding."

"May I ask you a question?"

"I can't wait," Elena smiled.

"Why did you stay?"

"What do you mean?"

"When your parents went back to America – why did you stay here?" Andrew asked.

"Do you need to see my residency permit?"

"No. I'm just curious. I'm asking for me, not as a policeman."

"So, this isn't you doing the serious interview thing. I wouldn't want to say or do anything inappropriate," Elena chided.

"I do occasionally have to actually do my job, you know."

Elena gave him a long look.

"I stayed because I love it here."

"I'm being serious," Andrew said.

"So am I. I love Scotland and especially the Highlands."

"But you're in the middle of nowhere!"

"So are you!" Elena replied.

"I had no choice. I was assigned here. It's my first posting."

"That explains a lot," Elena replied grinning.

"You think you're funny, don't you?"

"At least I don't wear my sweater inside out."

Andrew frantically tried to pull the back of the neck around so he could see where the label was.

Elena laughed. "Ha! Made you look! Why don't you go off and do some police work? I have to finish up my cleaning. You could give Helen a hand in the shed."

"That's a good idea. I'll go see if I can help," Andrew offered.

"There's wellies and heavy coats on the left before the side door. You'll need them."

Elena stepped on the ON button and the hoover whined back into action.

Andrew made his way through the kitchen and to the adjoining service area. He found a pair of boots that fit and an oversized anorak that didn't, then opened the door. He'd forgotten how deep the snow had become. Thankfully, either Leon, Helen, or both, had tamped down a makeshift path leading to the shed. He was glad for the boots and the coat. It was arctic!

Scotland in December on a stormy day could stay partially dark till noon or beyond. Andrew took extra care on the slippery surface, but still managed to fall on his arse a couple of times. Having finally managed the twenty-metre trek, he shook snow off his boots and coat then stepped into the shed. He ran right into Helen and Leon. They were standing stock still, staring at the butcher's table.

"What's wrong?"

"We seem to be missing something."

Andrew realised that the green tartan sheet wasn't actually covering anything any more.

Alan's body was gone.

"Where did it go?" Andrew asked.

"How the bloody hell should we know?" Leon barked. "Sorry."

"We came in to get a couple of legs of lamb for dinner and noticed that Alan seems to have gone for a little wander." Helen sounded stressed.

Andrew was at a complete loss. "But, where's his body? It didn't just get up and walk off." He suddenly had a thought. "Oh shit! He was dead, wasn't he?"

Leon looked at Andrew with concern. "You're joking, right? That was the deadest body I've ever seen. He was purple, for God's sake."

"Then where did he go?"

"We have no idea," Helen said. "Maybe someone's playing a trick on us."

"Who? One of the guests? Elena? First of all, I am the only one with a key; second, if you check outside there are no footprints or marks in the snow except the part we patted down, and finally, it took four of us to move him." Leon raised his palms in frustration.

"Have you checked the—?" Andrew gestured to the meat locker.

"First thing we did. Just the two deer we shot yesterday and the lamb we got from the Rankins' farm," Helen replied.

"What about the Rankins? Those two boys are always getting into trouble one way or another," Andrew offered.

Leon shook his head. "They're four miles up the road, and there's not a trace of a vehicle having been on the lane or our drive. They're as snowed-in as we are."

"So, what do we do?" Andrew asked.

"You're the policeman. You tell us," Leon snapped.

"I've been a policeman for seven months. My experience with dead bodies vanishing into thin air is a bit limited!" Andrew snapped back.

"That's enough, boys!" Helen sighed. "What we are going to do, is absolutely nothing. The poor man was already dead so it's not exactly a murder investigation, is it? We have six guests expecting to be looked after like royalty, so that is what Leon and I will continue to do. Hopefully, Alan will show up. In the meantime, I've got to put together a kedgeree for lunch and, Leon, the guests will probably start hovering by the bar soon. Once they've got drinks in their hands, you need to get on with making the mince pies for tomorrow. So, back to the house, all of you."

Helen and Leon toted the provisions back to the service door. Andrew stayed outside to have a quick look around.

What Leon had said about the snow being untouched was unfortunately accurate. Other than the newly trampled path, there wasn't any disturbance to the snow whatsoever. It was a pristine white cloak. Andrew pondered the idea that the falling snow could have covered tracks, but decided there would still have been some sign of them. Anyway, tracks from what? A walking corpse?

He made his way back to the service door and left the anorak and boots where he'd found them.

The guests were right where Helen said they'd be. Not exactly hovering, but in close enough proximity to the bar to be available for a 'wee dram' should Leon happen to appear.

Like meerkats, all six suddenly stood and stared towards Leon as he walked behind the bar.

"Can I interest anyone in a spicy Bloody Mary?"

The guests crammed into the tiny room. All had a hand in the air.

Andrew didn't want to disturb them so started to turn away.

"Not so fast, Constable!" Leon called. "You'll be needing one of these as well."

Andrew gave serious thought to declining but as he watched Leon prepare a pitcher of Bloody Marys with extra vodka, hot sauce, Worcester sauce and season salt, he almost started to drool.

Leon noticed and grabbed another glass from the shelf behind him.

The guests devoured their first drink in record time. Andrew was no exception. It took minimal persuading from Leon for him to whip up a second batch.

The guests filtered into the lounge and sat facing the fire as they started to tell hunting stories. Andrew listened while they boasted about their best kills and their hardest stalks.

"What about you, Constable?" Harry Stone asked. He was sixtyish, had a ruddy complexion and an astonishing head of almost white hair. It looked like it hadn't seen a comb in quite a few years.

"First of all, I'm currently off duty so, please call me Andrew. As for hunting stories, I'm afraid I have none."

The guests looked amazed.

"You live up here and you don't hunt?" Harry's wife, Anne, asked. She looked to be about the same age as her husband but spent substantially more time on her grooming. Her shoulder-length grey hair was carefully brushed and held off her face with a tortoiseshell clip. "Then what in heaven's name do you do for fun?"

"Mostly, I'm either working or studying. There's a lot of extra work to do for a first-year policeman."

"You must do something besides that. I mean something actually fun," Anne insisted.

"I like to run," Andrew offered. "Amazing trails and paths up here."

He could tell by their expressions that exercise wasn't considered something one did for fun.

"Was this your first dead body?" Cynthia Adams asked. Her voice was already developing a slight slur as a result of Leon's killer drinks.

"As a policeman, yes."

Douglas Adams jumped in. "What does that mean? Have you seen others when not being a policeman?"

He sounded as pompous as he had at breakfast. He already had a somewhat pointed face, but when intrigued, as he was then, he looked a little like a disgruntled weasel.

"I only meant that I haven't seen other dead bodies."

"I don't believe you," Douglas pushed.

Andrew studied the man with the vermin features. He could have let it slide, but he wanted to draw blood.

"You are very perceptive," Andrew said.

Douglas looked to the others in the room, proud of his achievement.

"I saw the bodies of my mother and father after an animal transporter crashed into them. I had to identify them once they were cut out of what was left of their car."

Andrew looked directly at Douglas. "Would you care for me to describe what they looked like?"

Douglas's head snapped back as if he'd been punched. His wife actually moved a few inches away from him.

"Please excuse my husband. He can be a bore and a prig. You've managed to meet him on a day when he's managing to be both." Cynthia offered Andrew a sympathetic smile. "Please accept my apology."

"There's no need. But, thank you. If you'll excuse me, I promised to give a hand in the kitchen."

He left the guests to wonder about the sullen young constable.

CHAPTER
SEVEN

Andrew wandered into the kitchen and found Helen busy preparing kedgeree for lunch, while Leon had taken over the kitchen table for his mince pie prep.

"Ah. There you are," Leon said. "I overheard a little of your conversation with some of the guests. I feel I should apologise for Mr Adams. He's a complete asshole."

"Can't argue that," Andrew agreed.

"They are still our paying guests, so please keep your character assassinations to yourself." Helen glared at her husband.

Andrew looked at Leon's carefully arranged ingredients for the mince pies. "I see you are making them the old traditional way."

"Well spotted. I thought it would be a nice change from the usual ones. Have you ever tried one?"

"Can't say as I have," Andrew replied.

"We'll bake some for the lunch sweet. You can sample one then."

"I'll have to pass, but thank you. Bit of an intolerance to white flour."

Leon studied his slight frame and nodded. "Your loss!"

"I made a vegetarian kedgeree for Elena or there's the traditional one with smoked haddock," Helen advised. "Which would you prefer?"

"How do you make a vegetarian kedgeree?" Andrew asked.

"I use mushroom instead of fish. It's more like a risotto."

"Actually, that sounds lovely. Is there enough for two?"

"There's enough for twelve," Helen smiled.

"Is there anything I can do to…?" Andrew began.

A loud yell from the lounge interrupted their conversation.

"I'll check it out," Andrew offered.

"That really would be a help." Leon gave him a thumbs-up. "My hands are nicely floured. Hate to wash them and start over."

Andrew returned to the lounge and found Douglas sitting on the floor looking dazed. Cynthia was next to him examining his right shin.

"Everything all right in here?" Andrew asked.

"Our friend appears to have had a bit too much vodka and tripped over the zebra – poor thing," Harry Stone answered trying not to smile.

"I did not trip. I was tripped!" Douglas insisted.

"When you say that you were tripped…" Andrew asked in his most professional voice, "… what does that mean?"

"It means that the bloody rug tripped me – intentionally!"

It was Andrew's turn to try and suppress a smile. "How exactly?"

"I was returning to my seat…"

"After sneaking off and helping yourself to another Bloody Mary!" Harry added.

"Having to be around you is reason enough for me to be able to have another drink if I so choose! Anyway, I was returning to my chair and was just about to step on the rug when it moved."

"Moved?" Andrew asked.

"Yes, moved. That bit there…" Douglas pointed at one of, what would have been, the animal's hind legs, "… flipped up and tripped me. I fell and twisted my ankle."

Harry smirked from the other side of the room.

"I don't see what you find so funny!" Douglas glared at him.

"Just enjoying watching you screw up as usual," Harry answered.

"Fuck off, you old shit. If I'd known you would be here, I would never have accepted the bloody prize."

Andrew looked to Cynthia for a translation. She just rolled her eyes, making sure her husband didn't see the gesture.

Andrew looked at the other guests. "Did anyone else happen to see this incident?"

"Now look here!" Douglas barked indignantly.

"It's my responsibility to check with possible witnesses at any accident site," Andrew explained.

He looked around the room but only received head shakes from everyone.

"May I ask how many Bloody Marys you've had?"

Douglas made a show of trying to remember.

Anne and Harry Stone both spoke up. "Four."

Andrew took a long breath then turned back to Douglas. "Is it possible you just tripped? They were very strong drinks, and as far as I can ascertain, the zebra does not seem to be in a suitable condition to have maliciously attempted to do you harm."

Douglas, with the help of Cynthia, made a big deal of getting to his feet. He looked towards the other guests. "Bugger off. The lot of you."

Cynthia helped him out of the room but not before looking back and mouthing, "I'm so sorry."

Once he was out of earshot, Harry mumbled, "Pompous git."

Everyone did their best to not laugh. They succeeded with the exception of Hilda Carter, who snorted before she could help herself.

"I just feel sorry for the zebra," Harry managed to say between peals of laughter.

*

The guests ate lunch in the dining room. Andrew ate in the kitchen. Helen's veggie version of kedgeree was delicious.

As he watched the others wait on the guests, he was amazed at just how hard the three of them had to work. If they weren't serving, they were preparing the next course or opening more wine or seeing to a guest's questions.

He would never have had the patience. Having to keep a constant smile on your face while tending to the needs of complete strangers wasn't his idea of fun.

It's not that he didn't have to maintain a professional air while dealing with the public, but he never had to act subservient.

"Can I help at all?" Andrew offered, feeling a little guilty watching them do all the work.

"You can get the mince pies out of the oven." Leon threw a tea towel at him. "Careful. They're hot. Elena, would you get the brandy cream out of the freezer?"

Andrew pulled out the industrial-sized baking tray and was amazed to see the rows of perfectly proportioned pies. They weren't the tiny store-bought mince pies. These were much bigger and sturdier looking.

"These look pretty good, Leon."

"Still can't tempt you with one?"

"'Fraid not," Andrew replied as he watched Leon place each pie on a cooling rack.

"Should be perfect in fifteen minutes. Helen, how's it looking out there?"

"They're about ten minutes from finishing their mains. We'll clear and give them a couple of minutes' breather then we'll serve the pies."

*

Andrew could hear the guests oohing and ahhing as the pies were brought out on a platter. It was The Lodge tradition (three days old), that the hosts join the guests for dessert and after-meal brandies.

After everyone was settled in the dining room, Andrew and Elena were alone in the kitchen. She grabbed one of the pies then dashed to the fridge and returned with her own tub of brandy cream. She put an enormous dollop of it on top of her pie.

She saw him watching with concern. "Your loss! Sure you don't want one?"

Andrew shook his head. He felt he should say something but decided to just let her enjoy her sweet. "I'll just watch you making a pig of yourself."

Elena reached across and punched him in the arm.

"I was wondering about the brandy cream. Is that part of a vegan diet?" he asked, rubbing the spot she'd punched.

Elena picked up the tub and held it up for Andrew to see.

"Cashew brandy cream," he read. "Suitable for vegan and non-dairy regimes."

"See! But thanks for the protective awareness. Is that something you Highland coppers do regularly?"

"Pretty much."

Elena forked a sizeable piece of pie into her mouth. Pastry crumbs cascaded onto the table.

"Delicious!" she managed to say with her mouth full.

"Nice table manners. Is that how you Yanks eat regularly?" he smiled

"Touché!" she mumbled through a mouthful of pie and cream.

She ate it all, then took another scoop of the brandy cream.

"To be honest, this is the real treat. The pie is just an excuse to eat more of it."

She started licking the semi-frozen cream off the spoon as if it was ice cream.

"Yum! Want a lick?"

She held the spoon out. Andrew, instead of licking, managed to suck the remaining cream right off the spoon.

"Aye. Not bad."

"You pig," she exclaimed.

"Careful! We'll have none of your derogatory American police insults."

They both grinned stupidly at each other until they heard a commotion in the dining room.

Walter Carter came charging out of the dining room. He ran through the hall where he had to battle the tree to get by. He then vanished out of sight.

Andrew stuck his head into the hallway and saw that Mr Carter had run into a large wet room at the back of the house. He was frantically unzipping a leather gun bag.

As Walter ran back past Andrew, he was inserting shells into the breach. He opened the front door and stepped out slowly.

"This can't be good." Elena had snuck up behind him. She did not sound happy.

She grabbed his hand and took him into the tiny morning room where he had carried out the interviews. She led him to the window. The view was spectacular. It was still snowing. The trees were laden with so much snow, their branches bowed under the weight. The entire vista seemed to be in black and white. The snowfall had somehow drained the world of colour.

Almost.

A single fawn and its mother were standing about a hundred metres away on a small hillock. Their legs were almost completely buried in the snow. They had found a few remaining berries on a low-hanging branch.

It was a perfect Christmas-card image.

Then it wasn't.

A single shot rang out. The doe's head snapped to the side as a fine red mist plumed outwards before the wind erased its presence. The doe toppled to the snow.

The fawn stepped over and looked down at its mother. It knew something was wrong. It sniffed at her then pushed her head with its nose to get attention.

Elena was frantically trying to get the window open. Andrew helped. They lifted the old sash frame and yelled out at the confused creature.

"Go! Run!" Elena screamed.

"Get out of here," Andrew cried.

The fawn seemed frozen in place.

Andrew started to crawl out of the window when they heard the second shot. Without even looking, he grabbed Elena and turned her away from the view.

Andrew watched as Hilda ran outside and joined her husband, as he stumbled through the snow to reach his kills. They were singing. The wind whipped most of their words away but it seemed to be Queen's 'Another One Bites the Dust'.

*

Andrew closed the window and took Elena into his arms. She was crying, her body shuddering against him.

The morning room door opened, and Helen walked in. Elena, seeing her, ran into her arms.

"How could they?" she cried.

"That's what they do. That's who they are. They know

that they're not supposed to shoot within sight of The Lodge but… that is why we are here."

"I know. I thought I could ignore it but… why? The locker has enough venison for weeks. They killed those two just for the fun of it." Elena was trying to dry her eyes on her sleeves.

Helen held her tight. "Yes, they did."

Andrew looked back outside and could see the Carters returning, the doe, over Walter's shoulders, the fawn over Hilda's.

Andrew stared at the happy couple as they stumbled back under the weight of their kills.

A deep-seated rage began to roil within him. Hatred coursed through his body.

CHAPTER
EIGHT

The other guests heaped praise on the Carters. Brandy was consumed and stories exchanged. Finally, they all drifted up to their rooms for well-deserved, alcohol-induced naps.

Leon and Helen had the extra task of cleaning and dressing the new kills. It was the last thing they had time for, but it was part of their function as hosts. They decided to let the two deer hang for a day before undertaking the task.

Once the venison was hung in the locker, they, along with Andrew and Elena, cleaned up the lunch mess and piled everything into the huge dishwasher.

Not a word was spoken during the entire process, though all eyes were on Elena to make sure she was coping.

Helen, aware of Elena's vegan lifestyle, had been worried about how she would react to being around hunting. So far she had handled it well. To see those bloody idiots shoot those two deer in front of everyone was uncalled for and clearly affected Elena deeply.

Helen had to wonder again, for the thousandth time, why they agreed to let the Carters provide the financial backing for The Lodge. Yes, the Carters owed them. They owed them a lot, but taking charity in the form of a partnership in The Lodge was just plain idiotic. They could just as easily have found a bank to loan them the money, or better still have gone back to doing what they did before they met the Carters.

What really upset Helen was that they had found a way to creep back into her and Leon's life. Not only that. They had become omnipresent. They had thoughts on the design, the furnishings, the food – everything.

Perhaps that was to be expected. What wasn't expected was how much she and Leon were learning to loathe the couple. They were rude, demanding, crass and soulless.

And those were their good features.

*

After that day in the cafeteria, Helen and Leon were inseparable. They studied together, took their A level exams on the same day and made love for the first time that same night.

They both passed. The exams and the lovemaking.

Leon was finally able to start work full-time. He was suddenly making real money. Peter began to put him on projects alone, letting him keep ninety percent of the profit for those jobs. In his first six months of working full-time, he had earned a whopping thirty-five thousand pounds. He had never realised how much a good plasterer could make.

He and Helen started making plans to rent a small flat so they could live together. Helen, being the more strategic of the two, suggested they instead buy a place. They could find a fixer-upper and flip it.

They stayed up all night working out the logistics of such a radical plan. The fact was the numbers added up. They had enough with Leon's savings to jump on the property ladder and by flipping one property a year, could make themselves a pretty good living.

A big part of their master-plan calculations was that they would use part of the savings as down payment. The rest was to fund whatever work needed doing to the property.

They just assumed that the banks would be lining up to offer them a loan. They never considered that the financial institutions would have a problem with their age. It was fine that Leon was making a decent salary as a plasterer, but neither of them was, as yet, twenty-one, and neither had any credit history.

They were devastated. Leon decided that their only option was to continue saving money from his earnings until they were deemed eligible for a loan.

Helen wouldn't hear of it. She knew that each year that one waited to buy one's first home, purchase prices would increase. She didn't want to keep chasing a dream that kept moving further out of reach by the day.

Helen considered asking for the balance of the money from her parents, but she knew the timing was pretty bad. Her father's cancer was in remission, but nobody knew for how long. It wasn't the time to be doling out loans to their daughter when he could be dead in six months.

She approached Leon about asking his father for a loan. He laughed. It was one of those 'you must be kidding' sort of *laughs. She knew all about the tension between father and son. On the one occasion she had dinner at their house, she got to witness it first hand.*

Leon's father treated his son with no respect whatsoever. No matter what Leon said, his father ignored him, belittled him or talked over him.

Helen fared no better. He talked to her as if she was a challenged child. He obviously considered the daughter of farmers to be way beneath his social standing.

She couldn't wait to get out of that house. She knew that no help would ever be coming from him.

Leon and Helen bandied around dozens of ideas, but nothing practical came to mind.

The next day when Leon headed off to work, Helen headed to the East End and found herself standing in front of Leon's family home. She had felt a wilful determination on the trip there. Now she doubted the very concept of her plan. Actually, there was no real plan. She just thought that maybe, if she and Leon's mum were able to have a chat without his dad being present, some idea would present itself. Now as she faced the door she realised that she had no business trying to circumvent the men of the family.

She started to turn away when the front door opened.

Leon's mother had seen her through the sitting-room window. The two sat for over an hour having a long chat about pretty much everything. Helen had no idea how to slip in the topic that had brought her all the way from Fulham.

Leon's mum was no fool. She knew exactly why Helen was there.

"Do you think it's time we discussed your reason for being here?" she asked.

Helen was so relieved she blurted out every aspect of their plans, including their complete failure to obtain a loan offer.

Leon's mum explained that, though she would be happy to lend them money, her husband was in charge of such things. She pointed out that he was about as likely to give them a loan as he was to start voting Lib Dem.

She did promise to have a word with him, but doubted he would agree to help.

As she held the front door open for Helen to leave, she smiled at her and gave her one parting thought.

"The one thing about life that you must never forget is to always have hope. Miracles do happen. Usually when you least expect them."

Helen felt at a loss as she stood in the rush-hour crush on the Tube home. She knew they were running out of options. She just didn't know where else to go for the money.

Two days later, a representative from Countrywide Building Society called and asked if they could stop by their Ealing branch to have a chat about a possible home purchase loan.

Leon's mother knew she never had a chance of prying any money from her husband, but he couldn't stop her co-signing Helen and Leon's loan. Especially if she never told him.

When they learned that they had been approved for a loan, they were completely gobsmacked. The pieces of their plan were suddenly falling into place. They decided to use twenty-five thousand as the down payment. The bank agreed to loan no more than eighty percent of the purchase price. That meant they had one hundred and twenty-five thousand pounds with which to find a suitable house.

They started the search the following day. It was a nightmare. The moment the London estate agents saw how young they were, they seemed to lose interest. It wasn't until they proved to each agent that they had the deposit and the loan guarantee that they at least deemed to show them property.

It took months. Any really great bargain was snapped up by existing developers – probably after a quiet exchange of cash with the agent. They always seemed to be one step behind everyone else at seeing the listings. They were getting more disheartened by the day.

After viewing a truly horrific little house in Wandsworth they were on their way home when they recognised one of the estate agents who had shown them a property the previous week. He had been extremely unfriendly and reluctant to spend any time with them whatsoever.

He was standing on the front steps talking to a well-dressed man in his forties. Leon and Helen overheard them discussing when to meet to sign the listing agreement.

They waited until the agent walked off, then approached the man as he started to get into his car.

They confessed to having overheard him speaking with the agent and told him that they were in the market and would love to have a quick look.

As no listing agreement had been signed and the agent hadn't shown them the property, he didn't see any conflict.

They spent over an hour with him. They liked the place. It was a complete mess, but with good bones.

It was a small three-bedroom, mid-terrace house just off Wandsworth Bridge Road. The Victorian home had been *used as student accommodation for the past twenty years and was an utter shambles.*

They needed another set of eyes to determine the extent of the work needed. The owner let Leon borrow his mobile flip-phone to call his boss.

Peter agreed to have a look before they placed an offer. When he wasn't plastering, he had a nice little side business as a home surveyor. He was only fifteen minutes away.

The owner was happy to wait and let Peter have a good nose around.

He slowly walked every centimetre of the place from roof to basement. He found so many issues his first pen ran out of ink. When he'd finally finished, the three huddled in a corner of the sitting room while he walked them through the list.

The good news was that there was nothing majorly wrong with the house. The bad news was that there were over one hundred issues that would need addressing almost immediately. There were early signs of rising damp. The roof joists looked to have woodworm. Half the floorboards definitely had woodworm. The plaster was blown in over half the rooms on walls and ceilings. The electrics were old enough to have been original. The kitchen cabinetry was staying together by willpower alone. The bathroom suite was cracked. Most of the old wooden-framed windows had swollen and couldn't be opened and the kitchen appliances were a fire hazard.

"So, is it a good house?" Leon asked him.

Peter took a moment to think, then gave them a positive nod. "Everything else is minor. Other than getting yourself some help with the electrics, I don't see why you couldn't do all the other work yourselves. Bottom line – it's a nice little home."

They approached the owner who had been on the phone in the kitchen trying to stay out of their way. The owner had wanted one hundred and thirty-five but after some hard negotiating and even a little pleading, he agreed to accept an offer of one hundred and twenty thousand. He decided that with the amount of work needed and the fact that he wouldn't have to pay a sales commission, knocking off ten thousand was only fair.

Leon and Helen had an accepted offer.

Two and a half months later, the sale completed and the couple were presented with the keys to their first house.

To save both time and money, they moved in the following day. They lived in the front room only while working on the rest of the house. It took just over nine months, but they finished all the work themselves except the electrics. Leon managed to barter with an electrician he knew. The sparks did the whole job for free in exchange for Leon re-plastering the interior of his home. A good deal for both.

The house looked almost brand new. They had painted every room a cheerful off-white that made the place seem bigger. They ripped up the old carpet and restored the wood flooring underneath.

It truly was a 'show' home.

They spent twelve thousand pounds of their own money bringing the total with purchase price to one hundred and thirty-nine thousand including solicitor costs. They listed it for sale at one hundred and sixty-five thousand. The house was shown eleven times the first day. They had four offers by the end of the second day. The estate agent ended up having to ask for sealed bids from the four interested parties.

The winning bid was for one hundred and seventy-three thousand.

Their gamble had paid off. They were able to continue flipping bigger and better homes until the day that they were invited to invest in a new-build project being developed by Walter Carter.

CHAPTER
NINE

Andrew found Elena alone in the morning room, dusting yet another mounted stag head.

"You all right?"

"Not particularly, but I'll get over it."

"I have to ask you again why you are here. I get the part about loving the Highlands and its people, but there's hundreds of different jobs that wouldn't require you dealing with hunting and hunters."

Elena gave him a resigned smile.

"When I heard what this place was going to become, I had this silly thought that if I stayed on I could maybe convert some of the guests away from killing for sport."

"I won't ask how that plan is working out."

"I have to keep trying," Elena stated.

"Isn't it just going to get harder and harder? I mean, the Franks have a lot riding on this place being a success. That means having lots of guests coming up here to shoot and fish," Andrew said.

"Kind of a crappy plan, huh?"

"Pretty much. Yes."

"Almost as bad as my parents' plan for the place," she sighed.

"A vegan meditation centre in the Highlands was a bizarre idea," Andrew remarked.

"Aren't you suddenly the font of all knowledge!"

"Most folks in town know about their B & B."

"They spent too much on the wrong location. Hopefully next time, they'll choose somewhere a little more accessible, and a little more amenable to trying something new," Elena said.

Andrew smiled. "This is the Highlands. They still consider pasteurised milk as something new. Veganism to them is simply incomprehensible. It's not that they're unwilling to try, they just don't understand the basic concept of why they should. To Highlanders, telling them they can't eat meat would be like telling cows they can't eat grass. They wouldn't understand you. It's not a conscious thing. It's simply a part of what they do and who they are!"

"So, basically you're saying they like meat?" She forced a smile.

She turned and started to dust the biggest trophy in the room. It was an entire stag's head with a mighty rack of antlers spreading almost the width of the mantelpiece.

"Where the hell did all these trophies and antler lights come from? I mean, Christ! There's a bloody elephant foot in here!"

"They bought them on eBay," Elena advised.

"I'm being serious. Where the hell can you buy this sort of dreadful stuff?"

"I take it you're not a hunter yourself then?"

"Never took to it. When we moved down to Yorkshire, my dad's new governor once tried to make me take part in a hunt. The ones with the dogs and horses."

"And a fox," Elena added solemnly.

"Yes. And a fox. I refused. I think he was quite embarrassed. He had hoped I could have been bloodied. In his world that was part of becoming a man."

"Is that when they wipe—"

"Yes. They wipe the blood from the dead fox on your cheeks."

"You English really are a little barbaric!"

"I'm Scottish."

"Then what were you doing living in England?"

"My father's work took him down there. We followed."

"Which do you prefer?" Elena asked.

"Scotland, but not the weather. There's only so much grey a person can take."

"I kind of like it. It's comforting. It's like the clouds are protecting us."

"What from – the sun?" Andrew joked.

"I can't describe it. I just feel safer away from everyone and sheltered under a big grey blanket," Elena explained.

"You are not completely normal, are you?"

Elena just shrugged and offered him a weak smile.

"Seriously, though." He stared up at the stag head. "Where'd this stuff come from?"

"I wasn't kidding. They found it on eBay. It was a bulk lot. Some hunting lodge in Yorkshire. I think the town was called something cute like – I remember – it was called

Newton-on-Ouse. I loved that name. Anyway, they were selling off everything."

"Why?" Andrew asked.

"They had some sort of accident and had to close," Elena explained.

"What sort of accident?"

"Apparently the kind where people die."

"What do you mean? How many people died?" Andrew asked.

"I have no idea. I didn't realise there'd be a quiz," Elena replied.

"Sorry. Force of habit."

Elena stopped dusting and stepped close to Andrew.

"You know, Constable, you ask a lot of questions."

She took a step closer. Their toes were practically touching.

Andrew took a nervous swallow.

"That's just what we do." His response might have been quite impressive, if his voice hadn't broken halfway through.

"Is that all you do?" Her voice sounded lower. More sensual.

"Well, actually…"

"For crying out loud, are you gonna kiss me or what!?"

Andrew seemed to consider the idea.

She rolled her eyes, grabbed him by his sweater and pulled him the last few inches.

She kissed him.

He kissed her back for a brief moment then stepped back, in effect ending the embrace.

"What's wrong?"

"Nothing. I just don't think it's the right time," Andrew replied.

"I hope you'll let me know when it's a more suitable time."

Elena punched him hard in the arm, then stormed out of the room.

A loud clanking sound suddenly started coming from the radiator. Andrew approached it and put his hand gingerly on its ridges. It was cool to the touch.

*

Leon was in the middle of making Yorkshire pudding batter so he could bake them later to go with the lamb. Not exactly traditional, but he felt that any meal could be improved with Yorkshire pudding.

The radiator in the kitchen suddenly rattled and groaned. He put the batter in the fridge then opened a utility drawer in the service area. He grabbed a torch, and a couple of tools.

The stairs down to the basement led off the wet room. He hated going down there. It was the only room in the house that had never been modernised. The stairs were the original rough-hewn, stone steps. They were uneven and awkward. The floor was also original. It was what the estate agent had referred to as quaint and unfinished. That was estate-agent bollocks for hard-packed earth with areas of protruding solid rock on which the home had originally been secured.

The basement was roughly a hundred square metres. The ceiling was low. Probably no more than two metres at the highest point.

At one end sat the building's original and still functional (usually) boiler. It was the size of the Mini Cooper that sat outside waiting for him to restore.

The only light in the space came from a strip that, no matter what Leon had tried, intermittently flickered and buzzed. Very little scared Leon, but there was something about the cramped basement that gave him a case of the willies.

Adding to the creepy vibe was that the basement was also being used as a temporary storage room. The balance of the hunting memorabilia they'd bought on eBay was down there. They'd had to buy the bulk lot to get the stuff they really wanted.

What remained in the basement was what was left over from the purchase. The remnants were wholly unsuitable for creating the atmosphere they were trying to achieve. There were dozens more mounted animal heads and bizarre antler lamps and ornaments, only these were in far worse shape than the ones upstairs. Another part of the collection that would never see the light of day were the taxidermic smaller animals.

There were squirrels, hares, rabbits, a fox, an owl, a falcon and one domestic cat. Some were mounted, others were freestanding. All had deteriorated badly over time. Their coats (or feathers) were soiled and had rotted away in places.

Leon had planned to burn the whole basement collection when he found time once the business was up and running.

Leon approached the boiler with trepidation. He was not a mechanical man by nature, but could usually work out how to finagle something into working again. This boiler however, was a whole different animal.

It had been built just after the Industrial Revolution by R. Jenkins & Co. It was originally coal-fired, but had been at some point changed over to heating oil.

It was too big to remove and too integrated into the house systems to easily swap out. For the most part, it worked like a champion. Occasionally, as if wanting to be noticed and pampered, it would glitch, rattling every pipe in the old manor.

Leon had been shown how to bleed pressure from a few different pipe junctions on the outside of the boiler. They were naturally difficult to reach, and could sometimes be hot enough to do some serious damage.

Leon turned on the overhead neon light, and true to form, it began flickering and buzzing as its worn ballasts tried unsuccessfully to balance the power load. Even with two neon bulbs, each over one and a half metres long, the unit hardly gave off enough light to see the surrounding walls. The light it did give was pale yellow. Leon planned to put a nice, cheery LED light array in its place, but that too, was pretty far down the list.

As he approached the boiler, Leon heard a scuffling sound coming from one of the piles of small stuffed animals. He knew they had rats down there, so wasn't that concerned. So long as they stayed away from the rest of the house, he would give them a little leeway in the seldom visited basement.

He turned on his Maglite and focussed the strong beam on the boiler. He traced the pipes to the first junction point. He cautiously felt the larger pipe. It was only just warm to the touch. He felt around till his hand came in contact with the first of the release valves. It was a brass cylinder with a finger-length bar fixed to the top.

Leon slowly lifted one end of the bar and immediately heard a loud hissing sound. Leon smiled. Hissing was good. It meant that air trapped within the sealed system was being released.

He continued to lift the bar until the hissing was replaced by a gurgling sound. He again felt the large pipe and could already feel heat increasing within.

He also heard a strange scratching sound from within the pile of antler lights and sconces. He shone the torch over at the pile but saw nothing amiss.

He moved to the other side of the boiler and repeated the same procedure with a different pipe junction. He was successful again.

When the hissing and gurgling stopped he distinctly heard shuffling from a completely different pile of eBay relics. This time it came from a mound of assorted stag head trophies. Something was moving within the pile.

Leon shone the torch but saw nothing but stag trophies and antlers.

He moved on to the final pipe junction and, having become a little cocky with his venting successes so far, he forgot to feel the main pipe first.

He stepped on the side of the boiler mount and went to reach back to the release valve. His arm came in contact with the pipe which, as luck would have it, didn't need venting and was scalding hot.

Leon screamed in pain, fell off the mount and landed face first on the basement floor. He watched as his Maglite rolled away from him across the uneven surface, bounced on a stone outcrop, then went out entirely.

"Fuck!" he shouted at himself for being such an idiot.

As he started to get to his feet, he sensed movement from the small stuffed-animal pile. The overhead light started flickering twice as fast. The effect was that of a weak yellow strobe.

He then sensed movement from the antler pile.

The illumination from the overhead neon stopped short of providing adequate light to the stored eBay items, so he couldn't see what was moving. He was encircled by shadows. The scuffling sounds were joined by a distinctive scraping noise.

The neon strobing became frenetic, flickering faster and faster until the ballasts failed and the basement was plunged into darkness.

Leon both heard and sensed things moving towards him from all sides of the basement. After a few moments of utter blackness, the boiler fired up sending a tiny ray of orange light from its view hatch.

It wasn't much light, but it was enough for Leon to see that the entire eBay collection had surrounded him. On one side, the small animals were all facing him less than a metre away. On the other side, the antlers and stag head trophies had also moved to surround him. They were upside down with their pointed antler forks acting as legs. Some were free-standing, others had their mounting boards now above them, looking like strange flat reptilian heads.

As he watched, he realised that only the ones not being observed, actually moved. When he focussed on the antlers, he distinctly heard the taxidermic menagerie shuffle a few centimetres closer.

He started to get to his feet and both flanks moved closer. Even in the minimal light from the boiler flame, he could see the small animals were no longer posed in what had presumably been intended as natural 'cute' positions.

They were now all in hunting posture. Their lifeless eyes seemed to sparkle by the fire's light. Their mouth and beaks, which were previously glued shut, were now open, revealing discoloured teeth and tongues.

As he stared at the creatures he heard the antlers scrape their way still closer.

"You all right down there?" Helen called from the top of the stairs as a swathe of light from the open door suddenly illuminated the room.

Helen saw Leon lying on the bare ground, curled up in a foetal position as he tried to swat something away from him. She turned on her jumbo emergency torch and came down the stairs.

"Stay where you are!" Leon yelled. "Don't let them get you too!"

Helen walked over to her husband and knelt beside him. "Honey? What's wrong?"

Leon slowly uncurled himself and looked around the room. The eBay items were all where they were supposed to be. The antlers and trophies were the right way up. The little animals were piled harmlessly against the wall. The neon overhead suddenly came back on. Seconds later his torch did the same.

Leon slowly got to his feet. Helen was looking at him very strangely. "What the hell happened?"

Leon looked around the basement. Had he imagined it? He dusted off his trousers and shirt then felt the burn on his arm.

"How did you do that?" Helen asked with concern.

"I think I must have pressed it against one of the hot pipes," he replied in a daze.

"Come on upstairs. I want to have a look at that. I think you might need some ointment."

Leon picked up his Maglite and followed his wife up the uneven stairs.

Just before reaching the top he heard a scuttling sound below. He looked back down, just in time to see the taxidermic house cat scamper from the shadows back to the pile of other little beasts.

He ran up the last few steps, slammed the door shut and double-locked it.

The basement light began to flicker again.

CHAPTER
TEN

The first thing Andrew saw when he walked into the kitchen was Leon's pallor. Helen was forcing him to drink what looked like a very large brandy as Leon looked straight ahead with a dazed expression. Every few seconds his left eye twitched almost comically.

"What happened?" Andrew asked.

"He came over a bit poorly in the basement. I think the carbon monoxide monitor may be faulty." She patted her husband's arm. "Come on. Drink the rest."

His eyes started to come back into focus. He looked around the room as if surprised to be there. "What happened?"

"I think you may have been breathing in carbon monoxide. I found you lying on the floor, swatting away at nothing."

Leon looked at her as if not understanding a single word she had just said.

"Why don't I go down and have a quick check? Do you have a spare portable monitor?" Elena offered.

Helen reached above one of the built-in cupboards and retrieved a small CO2 monitor alarm. She gave the test button a quick push. The room was suddenly filled with a banshee-like screaming alarm. Once it stopped, she handed the device to Elena.

"This one seems to work," she advised.

"So did my ears up until a few seconds ago," Andrew quipped.

*

Elena made her way carefully down the stone stairs then held the monitor above her head for over a minute. Nothing happened. She walked over to the boiler and did the same thing.

Satisfied that they weren't all going to die in their sleep, she turned to leave the basement. As she did she could see a ratty-looking stuffed squirrel tipped over on the dirt floor. The neon lights started to flicker.

"What happened to you?" She stepped over to the squirrel and picked it up gently and carried it back to the wall to join the pile of other little creatures. She then banged her palm against the ballast end of the overhead light. It stopped flickering and actually became brighter.

*

She reported back that all seemed in order below decks.

Andrew stood up from the table. "If you don't need

me, I thought I'd have a little poke around among Alan's things. There may be an address book or mobile phone. I might be able to find out who we should notify."

"I think the bigger problem is not who but how we're going to notify anyone." Helen looked out of the kitchen window. "The snow's the bloody problem. It's still coming down."

"It'll have to stop some time," Andrew offered.

"You're sure of that, are you?" Helen asked.

"I'm not," Leon added miserably.

*

Andrew went upstairs to his room and looked at Alan's belongings. There was one midsized rolling suitcase and one small overnight wheelie bag. They both looked well used but expensive.

He decided to start with the small one. He gently tipped the contents onto the bed.

There was a faux leather toiletry bag, a couple of paperback books that looked new, a guidebook for the Scottish Highlands, two boxes of Regal Game shotgun cartridges, a twelve-pack of Trojan condoms (unopened), a pair of glasses in a soft case, a pair of brogue shoes and at the very bottom, an iPad mini.

He opened it immediately. The home screen showed Alan in better times standing with two other men, each holding a brace of recently killed pheasant. He pressed the home button and the touch ID or passcode screen opened.

He stared at the ten buttons numbered 0 to 9. He didn't even bother trying. It was a recent iPad so it would require a minimum 6-digit sequence. Guessing was out of the question.

Leon hoped that Alan may have activated the touch ID.

He put everything back into the small wheelie bag except the iPad. He still had hopes of the man's body turning up along with his fingers. One of those would hopefully grant access to the tablet.

He moved on to the larger case.

It held fewer secrets than the small one. Sweaters, trousers, socks, underwear, T-shirts, polo necks and disposable hotel slippers from somewhere called the Royal Park Shiodome Hotel in Tokyo.

That was it. Andrew had hoped to find something that told a little more about the man. Then again, all of that sort of information was probably in the iPad.

He checked the wardrobe and found another brightly coloured dinner jacket, two dress shirts and two hunting hats.

Andrew felt along the shelf at the top of the wardrobe and found a hardback coffee-table book. It was a birdwatcher's guide to northern Scotland. Andrew flipped through it and was impressed by some of the beautiful pictures of Highland wild fowl. There were some stunning illustrations as well.

He was surprised that Alan, a hunter of winged creatures, would also be interested in birdwatching. Then Andrew noticed something very odd.

The author.

The book was written by Alan Hutchings. Andrew opened the back cover and sure enough, there was a photo of Alan drawing one of the illustrations.

Andrew was stymied. The man was clearly passionate about birds, yet was also perfectly happy to blast them out of the sky, then consume them with a little bread sauce and redcurrant jelly.

The man seemed very conflicted.

Andrew managed to fit both suitcases into the wardrobe. There remained no sign of the late Alan Hutchings. Bird lover extraordinaire.

He was able to breathe a bit easier with traces of the dead man out of sight. He stretched out on the bed and closed his eyes just for a few seconds.

Andrew thought back to his childhood in a house that was not that dissimilar to The Lodge.

*

Andrew had been born in a suburb of Inverness. They lived in a semi-detached three-bedroom home which backed onto open fields and a wooded area beyond.

His lasting memory of the house was that it was always warm and spotlessly clean. His mother had been emphatically house-proud. His father was an engineer in one of the many factories dotted around the city.

His salary was such that his mother didn't have to subsidise the household income and could instead focus on staying at home and making it a comfortable place for them all to live.

He remembered his father always finding ways to spend time with him. On the weekends, they were an inseparable team. His father tried to teach him how to fish and hunt, but little Andrew would have none of it. Not only did he refuse to hold a fishing rod or shotgun himself, he went out of his way to make noise and disturb whatever his father was trying to catch or shoot. After a few such sessions it was decided it was best that he no longer accompany his dad on such outings.

His was one of the only fathers he knew who not only played video games with his son but was bloody good at them too.

Andrew was a slight boy, prone to catching colds and coughs at any time of the year. His father had been determined to find a way to 'toughen' him up, no matter what.

He took him on long hikes on winter days. Andrew would always wake up the next morning with an awful cold. He tried taking him camping for two days during a rare spring heatwave. Andrew returned home with walking pneumonia.

His mother had, by that point, had enough of her husband's Dickensian methods of child rearing.

Under extreme pressure from his normally rational wife, he finally gave up with the 'toughening' plan. Even without his wife's mandate, he had started worrying that he would inadvertently kill the poor boy in an effort to make him healthy.

His father's biggest concern had been that being slight of frame and a sickly child, he would undoubtedly become a target for the school and even town bullies.

He was delighted that somehow Andrew never suffered from that particular tribulation. He had somehow found a way to talk to those who meant him harm into leaving him alone. It wasn't that he had any special powers, he was just able to defuse most tricky situations.

Andrew knew he could easily become prey to local bullies so he devised a defence whereby he distracted them by describing the psychological triggers that made them feel the need to bully.

Instead of being pounded on the spot, there was something about his mannerism and tone that made the other boys listen. They usually ended up asking him more questions, and even enquired if Leon had any suggestions about what to do about their condition.

Despite his almost constant ill health, Andrew remembered being a happy child. He liked his house, he liked his school, he was even beginning to like Martha Panning.

She was a year ahead of him in school, despite being a year younger. Andrew was never sure if she was extra bright or whether he was extra dim. As most of his classmates were the same age as Andrew, he went for her simply being a bit of a brainiac.

He'd had a crush on her for almost two terms, but he realised that she didn't even know that he existed. Then one spectacular Thursday, days before Guy Fawkes, she stopped him in the school hallway and not only addressed him by name, but asked him if he wanted to go with her to the fair that was setting up on the town common.

He walked home that night in a trance. He had visions of he and Martha marrying and living in a three-bed semi, just like his parents. The wonderful thing about being eleven was that all things seemed possible.

Andrew charged into his home, bursting to tell his parents the great news. He found them in the sitting room. The atmosphere was oppressive. He could see immediately that something was seriously wrong. Any thoughts of taking Martha anywhere became no more than a pipe dream.

Apparently, his father had just been advised that he was out of work. He and all his co-workers had been laid off.

The factory where his father had worked for twelve years had shut its gates permanently. It had had to close due to its manufacturing equipment needing an ever-increasing number of costly repairs. The machines were already obsolete by modern standard, but the owners had been perfectly happy to continue using them. That was until some of the bigger units started to fail. Repair costs suddenly went sky high. No matter how much creative engineering was used to keep them going, once they got to a certain age, things like metal fatigue became a real factor.

Refitting the factory floor with newer, more efficient equipment, would have cost more than the company's total appraised value.

One moment his father was a highly paid engineer, the next, he was out of a job with a family to support and a mortgage to pay. Like most people they knew, their family had hardly any savings put aside. They never felt that would be an issue.

His father tried to find suitable work locally, but had no success. He went to a number of interviews but came up against the same problem each time. He was a very skilled engineer, but on equipment built over fifty years earlier. He had no knowledge of the more modern computerised models with IP interface. He was a great engineer, but no one would give him a chance.

One of his laid-off co-workers stumbled across a company that was hiring in Yorkshire. They currently used some of the same machines that he had worked on in Inverness, but were about to stagger an upgrade to the latest models. The owner wanted to find engineers that knew the existing equipment, but who could also be trained up for the new ones. What's more, the company would pay for all the training.

His father called them immediately and was granted an interview.

Train service between Inverness and Skipton, the nearest station to the plant, required multiple train changes and was irrationally expensive.

He chose to drive the whole way, but with the family. He decided to make the trip an adventure, more than just a stressful interview trip.

They found a reasonably priced B & B on the north side of the town and a chippy only two streets away.

His father felt well rested the next morning when he presented himself to the human resources department of Harrington Manufacturing. He was made to fill out reams of different forms, then had to wait almost forty-five minutes before the engineering manager was ready to see him.

It turned out that the wait was worthwhile. They got on well from the start. His father's experience as a factory engineer, plus his degree in engineering, was exactly what Harrington's was looking for.

Andrew and his parents celebrated his new position by staying an extra night in Skipton. They splurged and actually went out for dinner at the Pizza Express just around the corner from the town hall.

The three devoured a plate of garlic dough balls, then each had their own individual pizza.

Andrew could still taste his La Reine pizza with chilli oil. The meal had been delicious and his parents had been visibly both happy and relieved.

That was a memorable time.

Andrew slept for almost three hours.

If Cynthia hadn't started screaming hysterically in the guest lounge, he might have slept right through dinner.

He forced himself awake then got shakily to his feet. He could feel the after-effects of the twin Bloody Marys. His head was throbbing slightly, and he could still taste the mushroom kedgeree. He stumbled into the bathroom and quickly brushed his teeth with one of the complimentary toothbrushes.

He ran downstairs and into the lounge. Cynthia was sitting in one of the leather armchairs. She was shaking and crying. The other guests were trying to comfort her. She looked to be in a right state.

"What happened, Mrs Adams?" Andrew asked gently.

"He was at the window. Just standing there when I opened the drapes. I wanted to check on the snow. He was staring right at me. Then he smiled. He smiled at me!"

"Who smiled at you, Mrs Adams?"

"His teeth – they were red. As if… It looked like blood."

"Who was it?" Andrew insisted.

Cynthia Adams looked up at the young constable as if he hadn't been paying attention.

"It was Alan. Alan Hutchings!"

"He was alive?" Andrew was stunned.

"God, no! He was very, very dead."

"But, you said he was standing there staring at you?"

"Because he was!" Cynthia answered.

"Then how was he standing?" Andrew prodded.

"They were holding him up. Lots of them!"

"Please, Mrs Adams. You're not making any sense. You saw a dead man at the window, and now you're saying people were holding him up."

Cynthia looked at him as if he was simple.

"Not people, Constable. Birds! Dozens of birds. All different sizes and colours. They were quite beautiful."

"That's enough." Douglas stepped between them. "I'm taking my wife upstairs to our room. She's had a terrible shock."

"Did you see Alan outside, Mr Adams?"

He looked even more like a weasel as he studied Andrew closely.

"No, I didn't. But poor Cynthia obviously did. I will not permit you interrogating her any further."

He helped her to her feet and led her out of the room.

Andrew looked to the others in the room and asked if they'd seen anyone at the window. No one had.

The guests returned to their rooms to dress for dinner, leaving Andrew alone in the lounge. He stepped over to the large window, and stared as far out into the night as the light from the room would allow.

The snow was still falling, but far more lightly. The wind had also abated. None of that helped his chances of leaving, as the snow was still at least one and a half metres high.

He looked down to where Cynthia had gestured that she'd seen Alan. The snow was untouched. There was no sign of anyone having been outside the window.

He was about to pull the curtains closed when something caught his eye.

A single dark feather sat atop the virgin snow.

CHAPTER
ELEVEN

The evening was less joyful than the hosts had hoped for. The Franks had planned for the Christmas Eve dinner to be festive, with lots of music, fine food and laughter.

They got the first two, but laughs were at a premium that night. Cynthia and Douglas had to be coaxed out of their room by the promise of homemade eggnog and roast leg of lamb, but their mood was strained and dark.

Cynthia was still very on edge after her earlier purported sighting, but there was something else. It looked to Andrew as if she and her rodent-faced husband had had a serious row.

The Carters were back to being their usual stoically unsocial selves, having exhausted all hunting tales earlier in the day.

That left the Stones. They tried everything to bring a little joy to the others in the lounge, but with minimal success.

Helen stuck her nose into the room and picked up the morose vibe immediately. She headed straight for the bar.

A few minutes later she returned, ice bucket in one hand, champagne glasses in the other.

"Who's for a little Bolli?"

She knew her audience well. Six pairs of eyes shot right to the bucket.

"Mr Stone? May I leave you to do the honours while I keep an eye on the lamb?"

"Absolutely!" Harry Stone took the bucket from her hand then skilfully uncorked the champers.

Once back in the kitchen, Helen helped Leon pull out the weighty roasting trays and basted the two lamb legs until they were glistening.

Andrew had again volunteered, but this time his offer was accepted. He sat at the big table, topping, tailing and stringing two kilos of green beans.

Opposite him, Elena was peeling sweet potatoes and carrots which were destined for high-heat roasting before becoming the main ingredients for the night's soup starter.

Leon's Yorkshire pudding batter was on the counter being brought up to room temperature before being baked to go with the lamb.

The operation was efficient and productive. The four made it look easy. Well, three of them did. Andrew's task could have been handled by a three-year-old. At least one with knife skills.

Helen stepped across the room and switched on the kettle.

There was a popping sound and the power went off. The guests theatrically moaned from the lounge.

Leon shouted, "I'm on it!"

A couple of plug-in emergency lights came on, offering a minimal amount of light.

"I think I just felt a squirrel on my foot!" Helen joked.

"Not funny at all." Leon was getting a little tired of her little jabs following his episode in the basement.

Leon found a torch, and headed into the hallway. He had to do some serious battling with the tree to get past it and open the under-stairs cupboard door.

He shined the light into the enclosed space. The master circuit breaker box was, for some sadistic reason, at the lowest point in the cupboard, closest to where the stairs met the floor.

That was the least of his problems.

When trying to find the most efficient location for some of the guest amenities just before opening day, Helen had commandeered the cupboard for the fishing supplies.

Normally that would be fine, but in the event of a power crisis, trying to move aside ten fly-fishing rods, six nets, six deep-water waders and ten folding fishing seats, was a complete nightmare.

Leon had to crawl into the cupboard on his hands and knees, then, making sure not to dislodge the fishing paraphernalia, turn sharp right and crawl under the underside of the stairs.

The only good thing was that Elena's parents had had the entire place rewired and the power meter, fuse box and distribution panel replaced. Why they didn't have it moved to somewhere accessible one will never know.

Leon managed to get to the fuse box. He opened the opaque plastic cover and saw that a secondary fuse labelled 'kitchen sockets' had tripped along with the master fuse for downstairs.

He flipped both back to the on position and could see light return to the hallway.

There was also a brief cheer from the lounge.

There wasn't room to turn around in the cupboard so Leon had to carefully crawl backwards to extricate himself from the cramped space.

Except he couldn't. His feet came into contact with one of the fishing nets. It toppled over knocking the others down with it. Leon tried to force his feet back but somehow became ensnared with one of the fishing poles.

He reached back to try and move it. He felt a sharp pain in his wrist. He'd snagged a hook free from the pole and managed to get it imbedded in his wrist. He felt panic growing within him. He tried deep breaths to calm himself.

He used logic and instead of moving backwards, went forwards as far as he could. Believing he was clear he shone the torch behind him.

Facing him was the giant stag head from the lounge. It took up the entire width of the cupboard. As Leon watched, its antlers began to move. The forks became pliant and seemed to be sensing the space around them.

Leon began hyperventilating. He tried to scream but couldn't. The head started moving towards him. Leon drew his feet up tight against himself convinced that he was about to die.

He suddenly had an idea. It wasn't much but it was all he had. He tripped the master fuse, then reset it. He kept flipping it up and down.

Though he didn't want to, Leon looked back over his shoulder. The stag was closer.

The cupboard door opened and Andrew's head suddenly appeared.

"Everything all right in here?" he asked calmly.

Leon looked back at him. There was no sign of the stag. However, he had managed to dislodge most of the fishing tackle and become entangled in it.

Andrew had to help remove all the paraphernalia from the cupboard then help pull Leon out feet first. The poor man was a wreck.

Andrew got him to his feet and was about to ask what had happened when Leon stormed out of the hallway.

He walked into the kitchen, opened a utility drawer and removed a roll of duct tape. He tore a small strip and placed it over the socket the kettle had been plugged into, all the while glaring at Helen.

She was trying not to smile, knowing that she had forgotten that that socket was off limits. It was just so handy that she kept plugging things into it, remarkably blowing the same fuse each time.

*

The guests made their way unsteadily to the dining room when Helen announced dinner.

After copious amounts of eggnog followed by the two bottles of Bolli (they had all wanted seconds), one would have thought that they'd reached their alcohol quota for the night.

Not by a long shot.

Helen had pre-opened two bottles of claret to let them breathe. She had expected those to last through the meal.

When she and Elena arrived to serve the soup with Welsh rarebit wedges, she saw that one bottle was already empty and the second was heading in the same direction. She whispered to Elena to please open another bottle and keep a fourth one on emergency stand-by.

By the time dessert, a Christmas-themed trifle, was served, the guests had managed five bottles. They were taking full advantage of the all-inclusive nature of their holiday package.

By the time they had consumed their after-dinner digestifs, they were all practically falling asleep in the lounge.

Helen and Leon gently suggested that they all call it a night and snuggle up in their beds before Santa arrived. Most agreed, but Harry and Anne asked for a small single malt each before calling it quits.

Amazed at their resilience, Helen poured them each a double and left them while she helped clean up the dinner debris.

*

The Stones each sipped their fifteen-year-old Scotches with suitable reverence. They held hands as they stared into the last embers of the fire.

Harry turned to his wife of twenty-two years and was about to make a disparaging comment about Douglas Adams, when he noticed something out of the corner of his eye.

He turned his head slowly, not wanting to spook it. It had gone behind the curtains, but he could see the material billow as it made its way to the other end.

He watched in drunken amazement as a moth-eaten-looking ginger cat slunk out from behind the curtains and moved towards the fire. Harry could see that one of its legs was hanging loosely from its body. It didn't seem to bother the cat in the least.

Harry turned to Anne but saw that she was out like a light.

He turned back to the cat and watched as it lay itself in front of the hearth.

Something else was moving behind the material. As Harry watched, a mounted stag head emerged. What Harry found most strange was that the head was upside down. The thing was walking on its antlers. Very well too.

He finished his single malt and observed the stag head untangle itself from the last curtain panel, then join the cat by the fire. The antlers parted in the middle, permitting the head to almost right itself. The head leaned into the cat as the two warmed themselves.

Harry thought it was one of the sweetest things he'd ever seen. He helped Anne to her feet then headed out of the room. At the doorway, he turned and took one last drunken look at the pair.

In a slurred whisper, he said, "Murry Cwithmath littew ones."

He helped Anne up the stairs and towards their room.

CHAPTER
TWELVE

Andrew was dreaming that he was at his police graduation ceremony. His parents were there with him, watching proudly from the front row. They were waving. His dad looked as proud as proud could be. His ma was crying she was so happy.

Andrew was crying as he slept. Even in his dream, he somehow knew that his parents weren't there. They had died years before that day.

As he stood on the stage, he was waving back at his parents but for some reason someone was shaking him.

"Andrew, wake up," Helen said. "Come on – we've got something to show you."

He tried to keep his eyes shut so as to keep the last tendrils of the dream alive.

To keep his parents alive.

"Andrew!" She shook him a little harder.

The fabric of the dream separated into a million

disjointed parts. Try as he may, he couldn't get them to reform into the happy image.

He opened his eyes. Helen was sitting on the edge of his bed, one hand on his shoulder.

"We need you to see something."

"This better be good." Andrew hardly recognised his croaky morning voice.

"I'm not sure that's the word for it." Helen left him alone in the room to throw on some clothes.

He caught up with her in the kitchen. They walked to the service area, donned outdoor gear and made their way to the shed. The snow had stopped completely but not before adding a good few slippery centimetres to the tamped snow pathway. It was just past seven on Christmas morning. It was still fully dark.

Helen led him into the shed. Leon was in the locker room, trying unsuccessfully to unhook a side of beef from the metal ceiling grid. Andrew stepped in to help, and grabbed the other side of the carcass and lifted. Both men were straining but without much success.

"I thought you were going to tell me that Alan had shown up," Andrew said.

"He did. You're holding him."

Andrew involuntarily let go and stumbled backwards.

"How do you know that's Alan?" Andrew asked.

Leon slowly rotated the hanging carcass. At the top, where the neck ended, was Alan's Christmas bow tie.

Repulsed, Andrew realised that the hanging meat was, indeed, Alan. Or at least what was left of him. He had been butchered. Butterflied to be precise. Cut down the middle, gutted and cleaned. His legs had been cut off at the knees, arms at the elbows, and his head removed at the top of the neck.

There was no blood. The body looked as cleanly butchered as any piece of meat he'd ever seen.

Andrew turned to Leon. His expression said it all.

"Don't look at me," Leon said. "I didn't do this. You and I together couldn't get him down. How do you think I could have got him up there?"

Andrew looked out past the locker door to Helen. She looked pale and shaken.

"Don't be daft! We didn't do this!" she said.

"Then who did?"

"No fucking idea," Leon snapped.

They both stood, looking at what was left of Alan.

"Could this be someone's idea of a joke?" Andrew said.

"Does this seem funny to you?" Leon said.

"Good point."

"I don't know how we're going to get him down," Leon stated.

"We can't bring him down. He needs to stay where he is till my people can get here."

"You must be joking. He's hanging next to our meat." Leon looked to his hands. "Christ. I need to clean myself."

Andrew studied the bizarre scene.

"Do you have any plastic sheeting?"

"Metres of the stuff," Helen answered as she entered the locker.

"Then let's leave him where he is, but wrap him up tightly with the plastic. That should alleviate the problem," Andrew suggested.

Leon shrugged a reluctant acceptance.

Helen looked like she wanted to ask something.

"What?" Andrew was pretty sure he knew what she was going to say.

"Can we still cook Christmas dinner?" Helen asked.

"Damned if I know," Andrew replied. "Amazingly, none of this was in my training."

He saw that the other two were looking hopefully back at him.

Andrew focussed on Helen. "Are you up to it? I'm sure the others would understand if you're not."

"Bollocks they would! They've paid through the nose for a Highland Christmas and besides, we can't afford to refund them at this point."

Andrew studied them both. He knew he should stop all festivities and re-interview everyone, but the man had been dead before the butchering. Besides, they were still legitimately snowed in. Nothing formal was going to happen forensically until the snow, or at least most of it, melted away.

He didn't fancy waiting the storm out with nine people who would happily hang him in the meat locker if their Christmas dinner was cancelled.

"To hell with it. Cook the bloody meal. It's not as if things could get much stranger," Andrew announced.

"May I suggest that we don't mention this to the guests?" Helen said.

"I agree. The last thing we want to do is cause a panic," Andrew agreed.

*

The three wrapped Alan's hanging carcass in sheets of clear plastic, three layers deep. Helen then instructed the two men to fetch the geese from the back refrigerator so she could prep them for roasting as soon as they'd finished the breakfast serving.

They laid the two birds on the prep bench next to the butchering table. Helen knew that she was going to have to give that table a serious scrub down before using it to prep the birds. She grabbed a box of lye and shook a thin film onto the wooden surface. She planned to let that sit for an hour before going at the table with hot water and a wire brush.

*

They'd prepped most of the breakfast earlier in the morning so it was just a case of frying up the last-minute things like bacon, eggs, sausages and toast.

The spread was similar to the previous day's except, being Christmas, they went all out. They'd added kidneys, fried bread and baked beans. It was the best British fry-up Andrew had ever seen.

The guests came staggering down shortly after the last entrée dish was in place.

They unsurprisingly looked a little worse for wear. That didn't stop them, however, from eating an astonishing amount of food.

Andrew stayed in the kitchen and nursed a large bowl of porridge with raisins, brown sugar and heavy cream.

Before anyone else had finished, the Carters stuck their heads into the kitchen.

"We're going out."

Leon looked at them incredulously. "Where to? The snow's too deep to walk anywhere."

"We'll be fine. It's our little tradition to have a quick shoot Christmas morning."

They headed to the wet room at the back of The Lodge and removed their scoped rifles from leather cases. The Carters then checked that their rifle magazines were full and that they both had a few spares just in case. They donned heavily padded shooting jackets and hunting hats with fold-down ear flaps.

Hilda and Walter opened the back door and stepped out into what most would have considered a winter wonderland.

They considered it a potential killing field.

They strode, side by side, through almost waist-high snow. They weren't deterred in the least. The going was tough, but nothing was going to stop them having their Christmas shoot.

They walked through The Lodge property, then up a gentle hill and down the other side till they reached a small copse of old-growth downy birch. They chose that spot as their hide. They stood between the dozen or so trees and waited.

There was no rush.

They were willing to wait all day for the right kill.

*

Once the couple exited the back of the house, Andrew turned to the Franks.

"Is that normal behaviour?"

Leon tried to force a smile. "In case you haven't noticed, normal behaviour appears to be in short supply this Christmas."

At that moment, Harry stuck his head round the kitchen door. "I have a strange question. Do you have a cat? A slightly ratty orange one?"

Leon dropped a plate he was about to place in the cupboard.

Helen rolled her eyes. "We don't have any pets. Why?"

"Actually, that's a big relief. It means I dreamt the whole thing," Harry said.

"Dreamt about what?" Leon tried to keep his voice calm.

"Nothing. Just too much rich food and eggnog. Terrible combination." Harry headed back to the dining room.

Helen was looking at Leon with real concern. "What's the matter, Leon? You've gone all pale."

"I may be going insane."

"Oh, my dear love," Helen said. "That ship sailed years ago."

"I know you don't believe in this stuff but I feel that something weird is happening at The Lodge," Elena said.

"You do realise that you say that about once a week?" Helen smiled over at Elena.

"I know, but this time the feeling is much stronger."

"Actually, if I may put my two pence in," Andrew explained, "I think what we are suffering from is good old-fashioned cabin fever. This is the third day of being cooped up inside. That would send anyone a bit batty."

They all nodded tacit agreement.

"Possible, but I still feel something in my gut," Elena insisted.

"That could be yesterday's kedgeree," Helen said. "Anyway, I'm off to give the butcher's table the scrub of its life. You lot finish up with the clearing when the guests retire to their rooms. Elena, try to do a quick clean in the lounge if you can, and Leon, please see to that blasted tree. It's still bloody growing."

"What about me?" Andrew asked.

"You can act like a guest this morning. Go and have a nice hot shower and do whatever you usually do first thing in the morning."

With instructions given, Helen donned her arctic gear and stepped out of the side door.

*

Andrew stood under the steaming shower and held his face up to the spray. He felt relaxed. It was Christmas Day and for a change, he wasn't alone.

*

When he was younger and his parents were still alive, Christmas was a big deal to his family. His mother would sit glued to every TV ad from the big supermarkets, and write down all their newly created Christmas recipes.

Dark chocolate and ginger Christmas pudding. Roasted chestnut with dried cranberry and brandy stuffing. Whatever it was, she wanted her family to partake.

They started Christmas feasting as early as the 15th December and ended the binge on 2nd January.

Buying the tree was another extravagant indulgence. For someone who spent the rest of the year being frugal and sensible, his mother morphed into a raging consumer over the holidays. She wasn't satisfied with a manageable two-metre tree like most of her friends. She would shop until she found one that would just miss the ceiling once the angel was on top, by a centimetre or two.

The end result of her brief annual shopaholic spree, were fantastically memorable Christmases. They would eat till they couldn't move, sing along to every Christmas song on radio, decorate every part of the house imaginable – inside and out – and watch every single Christmas movie on TV.

Those Christmases would stay locked in Andrew's mind forever.

Especially their last one.

*

Andrew was fast asleep Christmas morning up until the moment his mother shook him awake. He glanced at his clock and saw that it was only 6:00 a.m. His mother had seen a late-night local TV ad announcing that Santa's Village Store would, for the first time ever, be open from 7:00 a.m. to 10:00 a.m. on Christmas Day! Not only that, but all the Christmas stock would be on sale for seventy-five percent off.

He had never seen his mother so excited. She was actually giddy.

Andrew managed to dress and stagger downstairs where his father, looking just as sleepy as Andrew felt, was waiting by the front door.

"No breakfast?" Andrew asked.

His father replied, "Apparently not. Your mum wants to be the first one there."

"But I'm hungry."

"Join the club, mate. Hopefully they've got some food at the shop."

His mum charged through the hallway and opened the front door. "Come on, lads. Can't be late."

Andrew and his father shared a brief, knowing glance.

It was sleeting as they ran for the car. The weather report had promised snow, but it was a few degrees too warm for that. They bundled into their bright blue Vauxhall Astra, and were greeted with Christmas carols the moment the car started.

"Come on then," she said. "Ten points to the person who gets all the words right."

She always won.

The roads were almost devoid of traffic. Most of England stayed put on Christmas Day. Still, even with empty roads, it would take almost an hour to get there.

They joined the A1(M) at Wetherby, then headed north to Boroughbridge where Santa's Village was located. With Slade music blaring and Christmas spirit at peak level, they turned onto the off-ramp for exit 48.

Andrew never knew if his father saw the lorry or not. It wouldn't have mattered. The animal carrier was out of control and going too fast the wrong way to have reacted.

It was half on, half off their exit ramp. The driver tried to miss their car but only succeeded in making matters worse. The lorry broadsided the front half of the Astra, tearing the small vehicle in half.

Andrew remembered that he was singing along to Slade's Christmas song. The next moment, he was looking down the embankment through the open front of the car. There were no front seats, no dash, no windscreen, nothing. Just open air.

He managed to undo his safety belt, but couldn't open his door. It took a few moments for him to realise that he didn't need the door. He could just step forward.

His ears were ringing yet he could hear his own heartbeat. He didn't know where he was. He was dizzy and felt nauseous, but knew he had to keep moving. There was something he needed to find.

He got to the ramp and saw the back end of the animal carrier sticking up in the air at an odd angle. The lorry was facing down the other embankment. Its tail lights were on, and its left-hand signal was flashing.

The most surreal memory was the sound of the animals. They were screaming.

Andrew crested the embankment and walked along the side of the carrier. The entire vehicle was somehow twisted. Its front had rotated almost forty-five degrees from the back end.

The carrier pen had split open in numerous places. Dead cows hung across the aluminium siding, some almost completely cut in half. Others had grotesque injuries yet were still just alive. Some lucky few had either been thrown clear, or had found a way out, and were peacefully eating grass by the side of the wreckage.

Andrew made it to the cab, or at least what was left of it. The motorway retaining wall had stopped the lorry. But not before the impact had crushed the cabin to less than a quarter of its previous size. Whoever had been inside would not have survived.

Dazed, Andrew walked back around the rear of the vehicle and down its other side. The animal carnage was even worse. Andrew could see that the carrier hadn't only been transporting cattle. Pigs had also been on board and had faired just as badly, if not worse, than the cows.

Andrew had to walk around whole, and partial animal carcasses. The embankment was sticky with blood. Their cries and screams filled the air.

Andrew finally found the front remains of their family car. It was smashed up against the retaining wall less than a metre from the lorry. Smoke was pouring out of the wreckage. He couldn't tell if his parents were still in the car. Like the lorry cab, the car had been concertinaed against the wall.

Black smoke was pouring from every opening.

Under the harsh glare from the motorway lights, Andrew could see a few parts of the car's cheerful blue paint job – the parts that weren't covered in bovine blood.

Andrew was surrounded by dead or dying animals. Though he was in shock and feeling very little, he sensed some force bonding them together. It was as if the dying creatures were sending their final life-essence towards and through him.

*

Andrew was found by the first responders. He was sitting on the blood-soaked grass, nearly comatose, staring vacantly at the gore-speckled retaining wall. He was still singing Slade's Christmas song.

CHAPTER
THIRTEEN

Leon finally decided to tackle the mysteriously expanding Christmas tree. He walked into the hallway, fully equipped to do battle. He immediately saw that the tree was bigger. Not taller, just wider and fuller.

He reached between the branches to feel if the trunk itself had grown. As he stretched within the dark recesses, he felt something drop directly onto his head, bounce, then land on the cotton wool faux-snow at its base.

He withdrew his arm and looked down. A gold-coloured orb sat unbroken at his feet.

He took a step back to take in the tree as a whole.

He noticed that another bauble had started rocking in place on a higher branch.

This time the bauble didn't simply drop. It flew off the tree and headed straight for Leon. It hit him on the right cheek and shattered. Leon, stunned, reached up and felt a tiny rivulet of blood running down to his chin.

"What fresh hell is this!?"

Another orb flew at him. He managed to duck. He wasn't as lucky when the next volley headed his way. Six baubles and a tiny ceramic Santa hit their mark. Head, neck and arms.

He was now bleeding from multiple tiny cuts.

Ignoring the assault, he stepped into one of the larger branches and deftly cut it cleanly off, near the trunk.

The other branches began swiping him from all directions. Decorations flew everywhere. Christmas lights began flickering rhythmically, almost pulsating, as he cut another branch.

One strand of the lights rose from the tree and coiled above it. As Leon continued his frantic pruning, it dropped, encircling his neck. It began to tighten. Another strand wrapped itself around his right arm.

Somehow, in the midst of the nightmarish insanity that had enveloped him, Leon knew that the one thing he mustn't do was to give up.

He leaned into the tree with all his weight, and managed to shift it off balance. Even as the wires tightened, he kept pushing.

The tree started to topple. It fell onto the hardwood floor practically filling the entry and the main hallway.

Leon cut the LED cable around his neck, receiving only a small jolt of electricity. Thankfully the strand's transformer reduced the voltage for the tiny lights. The shock was more like a fizz than a real shock.

That done, he began cutting anything he saw – wires, branches, tinsel. Everything and anything.

The tree stopped fighting back. By that point, it had no arsenal left with which to defend itself.

Leon, exhausted, lay amidst the mass defoliation, trying to catch both his breath and his sanity.

Then he heard it.

Something was making its way down from where the top of the tree would have been, had it still been vertical.

He couldn't make out what it was until it stepped clear off one particularly large severed branch. Even then, though completely visible, his mind couldn't fully wrap itself around what his eyes were seeing.

The tree topper – an antique carved ivory angel that his mother had given them for their first Christmas together, was crawling across the pine needles towards him.

The miniature Victorian lace gown was no longer a pristine cream and gold. It was torn and stained with sap. The angel's bouffant hair was straggly and stuck to one side of her face with the same pine sap. The scariest part, if Leon had to choose just one, was its mouth. The gentile, angelic smile was gone. Its lips were parted. Tiny yellow pointed teeth were gnashing up and down as it scurried towards him across the bed of severed branches.

Leon had no idea how he reacted as he did, but in one reflexive move, he grabbed one of the Christmas light cables and tore off the transformer then jabbed the frayed copper wires right into the angel's face.

Without the transformer, the angel got the full two hundred and twenty volts. More than enough to ignite the sap on its face and hair.

It started to burn. Slowly at first, then the antique lace lit up like a magician's flash paper.

The angel's clothing burned to ash in seconds.

As Leon took a relieved breath, he saw to his horror

that the angel, now naked and charred, was still crawling towards him. Parts of it were still smouldering, sending out the occasional spark. What was worse was that its charred, ivory body was making a high-pitched squeal as it expanded under the intense heat.

Leon brought the shears down on either side of its neck, and snipped. The blackened head fell to the side, and the rest of it dropped, unmoving, to the bed of needles.

Andrew chose that moment to walk into the hallway.

"Jesus Christ, man! I offered to help. I thought you were just going to give it a wee trim."

"Fuck you!" Leon replied as he tried to disentangle himself from the remains of the festive fir tree.

"Feel like telling me what happened here?" Andrew clearly found the sight amusing.

"What would you say if I told you it fought back?" Leon asked.

"I'd say that we might have to consider having you sectioned."

"In that case, I have nothing to say. I will however accept your help in tidying up this bloody mess!"

"That I can do."

"Make sure everything is dead!" Leon advised.

Andrew gave the other man a very concerned look.

*

While the two were trying to bin the tree debris and get it moved out of the hallway, Douglas Adams descended the stairs and gave the two a puzzled glance.

"Just had enough of the bloody thing!" Leon quipped. "Can I help you?"

"Cynthia was wondering if there was a chance of any more tea?"

"We left the coffee and tea set-ups in the dining room," Leon said. "I put out some slices of chocolate Christmas log. Try some. It's delicious."

Andrew could have sworn that the man's nose started twitching at the mention of more food.

Leon and Andrew finished the hallway clean-up. Despite repeated questioning from Andrew, Leon refused to discuss what had happened and instead, went off to start prepping the veg and Christmas pudding.

Andrew went wandering. He told himself that he was just familiarising himself with the property, as any responsible policeman would do.

His real quest was to accidentally bump into Elena. He knew he should be a hundred percent focussed on his job, but there was just something about her.

It was a very quick search. She was back hoovering away. As he watched from the doorway, she finished the hoovering and started dusting the tables and mounted hunting trophies. She was wearing a light blue dress that came down just below her knees. As she stretched to reach the higher parts, her skirt rode up her shapely legs. Andrew tried not to notice.

He failed miserably.

"Doesn't that bother you?" Andrew asked as he entered the room.

"Why should it?" she replied. "It's my job. Besides, these poor animals are already dead. I get more upset with the killing of the live ones."

"Mr and Mrs Carter are out there right now planning to shoot something."

"I know," Elena said. "I wish the animals could shoot back. Now that would be interesting."

"What happens to you if things don't work out here?" Andrew asked.

"Why wouldn't things work out?"

"I saw the effect that those deer being shot had on you. Do you really think you can stand being around that every day?"

"Don't forget," Elena said, "I plan to find a way to change people's minds about the killing."

"I don't think you realise how hard that's going to be. People who hunt, love to hunt. It makes them feel powerful. How are you going to talk them out of that?"

"One baby step at a time," Elena smiled. "Maybe I'll think of another way at some point, but I have to start somewhere."

"When all this is over – perhaps..."

"When what's all over?" she interrupted. "You mean Christmas?"

"Of course. What else could I mean?" Andrew replied.

"I'll have to check my calendar," she continued. "I assume you were about to ask me out?"

Andrew gave her a dumbfounded look.

"I may be able to fit you in sometime in January," Elena said. "February at the latest."

"Let me know." Andrew started to walk away while shaking his head in amazement at the girl's cheek.

"Where are you going?"

He turned back to face her just as she stepped into him. The kiss was quick but enough to start him blushing again.

CHAPTER
FOURTEEN

Helen finished scrubbing the butcher's table and was giving it a final rinse. She was exhausted. Her arms ached and she could still smell disinfectant and lye in the air.

She wished she could make the guests some sandwiches for lunch and call it a day, but it was Christmas, and they expected, no, demanded a full-on holiday dinner.

She'd initially been worried that they'd balk at having goose instead of turkey. She had convinced them that, as Scotland had no wild turkeys, a brace of Greylag geese would be far more flavourful and in keeping with The Lodge's game philosophy.

She had picked the best two from a farm in town on the 23rd. They had been slaughtered by slitting their throats and were then plucked. The geese were kept intact so that the gaminess could be enhanced after two days of hanging.

Helen sharpened her cleaver and prep knives, then laid them in order of use on the butcher's table.

She hoisted the first bird onto the work surface, stretching him out to full length. She lifted the cleaver and brought it down on the exposed neck. Or at least that was the plan. She missed. She knew she was tired but still, this was hardly precision work.

She lifted the cleaver again and, holding it with both hands, brought it down in a fast arc. She missed again. She looked at the bird then the cleaver and for the life of her couldn't work out what was going on.

She tried a couple of practice chops further along the table and was dead-on accurate.

She turned back to the goose. She took a deep breath then exhaled completely. She raised the cleaver, her eyes glued to the bird's neck and head.

She was about to chop when the goose opened its eyes. It stared straight at her. Helen gasped but continued anyway and started to bring the cleaver down.

A sharp pain in her calf caused her to miss the neck entirely. She looked down and saw that the second goose was standing next to her with its beak clamped onto her leg.

She tried to kick it away but it side-stepped and bit her ankle, drawing blood. Helen grabbed her long carving knife and swung it at the attacker.

The goose on the table chose that moment to clamp down on the back of her neck. Helen dropped the knife in shock. The other goose stood tall. Its head reached Helen's midriff. It started pecking anywhere it could see flesh.

Helen tried to grab the knife, but the moment she bent over, the bird went for her face. The other goose jumped on her back and continued to bite her neck.

Helen started screaming.

She managed to shake the one off her back and planted a pretty good kick at the bird on the floor.

She backed away as the two Greylags followed her, snapping at the air between them. Their neck skin flapped open and closed where their throats had been slit. Helen was forced against the shed wall as the two geese narrowed the distance between them.

Helen felt along the shed wall while keeping her eyes on the wild fowl. Her hand found what she'd hoped would be there. She swung the powered tree trimmer in front of her and pulled the starter cord. It coughed once. She realised she hadn't turned the fuel-line valve. As she looked for the tiny plastic knob, the geese reached her.

She found the knob, turned it, and pulled the cord as the geese started biting her legs.

The trimmer's motor fired. She revved it once then took aim at the first bird.

*

Leon was frying up onions for the stuffing. His arms were a mass of plasters covering the battle scars from the tree. Andrew was on spud-peeling duty and Elena was on sprouts.

Helen stormed into the kitchen and slammed down the two geese. They were oven ready, cleaned with feet and heads removed. Leon looked at them in shock. The goose flesh was scored and slashed in numerous places.

"We can't serve those," Leon exclaimed. "What happened to them?"

He noticed that she was bleeding from dozens of bite marks. He stared at her in complete shock.

"Don't be such a pussy!" Helen said. "Just put bacon over the cuts. They'll never know."

She then noticed all his plasters. "What's your excuse?"

"The tree fought back."

"There's a lot of that going on at the moment," Helen replied.

Leon looked at her with real concern. "Want to tell me about it?"

"No. How about you?"

Leon shook his head. "No. Not today. We can get into whatever the hell is going on once the guests are gone."

"Right then – let's get this bloody dinner going," Helen said.

Elena and Andrew gave the Franks worried looks, but continued their vegetable duties.

A few minutes later, Douglas Adams stuck his head into the kitchen.

"If you're not too busy, a Christmas cocktail would be rather nice." He forced a rodent-like grimace and headed back to the lounge.

Helen mimicked under her breath, "If you're not too busy...! I'll give you 'not too busy', you pompous..."

"Your charm is showing, darling," Leon said. "I'll get the guests some Black Velvets then finish up in here. The chestnut and brandy stuffing is done and is over there on the counter."

Leon washed his hands and headed for the bar.

"Black Velvet?" Andrew asked.

"Guinness and champagne," Helen advised.

"Sounds like a terrible waste of Guinness."

"And champagne," Elena added.

"We use cheap naff champagne for that. But I agree about the Guinness," Helen said. "Oh, I just remembered – Elena, please tell Leon that the Carters are still out shooting so he only needs to make four drinks."

Once Elena was out of the kitchen, Andrew asked, "How did you get involved with the Carters?"

"Don't you mean why?"

Andrew laughed. "You do make unusual bedfellows."

"What a disgusting thought," Helen said.

"It was just an expression."

"I know, but still—" Helen was stuffing both ends of the goose with none of the care one would associate with fine cuisine. She looked like she really meant it.

"Leon inherited some money after his mum died and we wanted to invest it together with the savings we'd made from our property business. We made a nice tidy sum over the years flipping houses. We felt the time was right to have the money do all the work instead of us.

"We spoke to some friends and that led to our meeting with a venture capitalist. He had a couple of good investment opportunities coming up. The best was buying into a new construction project. A new estate, with thirty-two new-build homes just outside Reading in Berkshire. Walter was the developer. We were told to expect a fourteen percent return once all thirty-two homes sold."

"That must have been nice," Andrew said.

"It would have been. Unfortunately, that was in 2008."

Andrew gave her a questioning look.

"That was when the housing market crashed."

"Ouch! Not a good time for investing in property," Andrew replied.

"Not for us. We started a whole new investment model – buy high sell low. It took almost ten years to sell the last house."

"So, you did eventually get paid?" Andrew asked.

"No, we did not. After the crash, nothing sold for years, then after slashing prices, a few were bought. By the end, the homes went for less than cost. We never made a penny," Helen said.

"I hope you got your original investment back?"

"You're looking at it!" She gestured theatrically at the surrounding walls.

Andrew grimaced. Partly at Helen's story, but also at the force she was using on the second goose as she forced chestnut stuffing into its body cavity.

CHAPTER
FIFTEEN

Andrew was taken to the nearest A & E to be evaluated. By some miracle he had sustained no injuries whatsoever – physically. His mental condition, however, was another story altogether. He remained partially catatonic for over a month. Every waking minute, he just sat next to his bed in the dreary ward, staring out of the window at the fields beyond. He seemed most focussed on the animals grazing in the distance.

Despite many hours with mental health professionals trying to bring him back to the real world, Andrew wouldn't talk. What he would do, at random times, was sing Slade's Christmas song.

It wasn't until weeks later when a local charity brought a golden retriever puppy into the ward that things changed.

Andrew was, as usual, staring at the fields when the puppy walked right up to him and began licking his hand. Andrew looked down at the young dog and suddenly started to cry. He knelt next to the animal and buried his face in its shiny coat, all the while sobbing quietly. The dog never moved.

When the handler tried to gently pull the dog away, the puppy pulled back and wrapped itself under Andrew's legs. The puppy stayed there until Andrew stopped crying and stood up. He looked around the ward as if seeing it for the first time. A nurse came up to him to see if he was all right. He looked up at her with red-rimmed eyes.

"Are Mummy and Daddy in heaven?"

*

Andrew's only living relative was his grandmother, Ruth. Though in her late seventies, she was happy to bring her grandson into her home.

She lived just off the M4 a mile outside Datchet. She had lived in her tiny two-bed cottage almost her entire life. When her husband originally purchased it, there hadn't been another house within sight in any direction.

Things had changed in seventy years. Private and council estates had popped up everywhere. She ended up with neighbours only a few hundred metres away. Thankfully, each of those homes had been built on an acre of land so she still had some of the feel of living in rural countryside.

Andrew celebrated his twelfth birthday one week after moving into the cottage. Ruth had a few of her friends over and had bought a nice little cake from the Co-op. There was a time when she would have baked one herself, but since her arthritis had worsened, shop-bought was her only choice.

Andrew's days consisted of taking the bus to his school, doing a bit of shopping afterwards then returning to what *was now his home. He made friends with Ruth's ancient and bad-tempered cat, Pepper, and took over most of the chores that were needed to maintain their little home.*

He thought of his parents every moment of the day but the pain slowly evolved from a soul-wrenching agony, to a dull, constant ache. They were in his dreams every night. Some were wonderful and almost soothing. Others woke him, screaming.

Things quickly got into a routine. He made some schoolfriends and Ruth seemed healthier and somehow younger with a young person in the house. Andrew knew that things could have been much worse.

*

Then the first letter arrived. It was from a solicitor in Reading. It was an offer to buy Ruth's cottage. The price was above market. Ruth just laughed as she crumpled the letter and tossed it into the recycle bin.

The second letter arrived one week later and, though basically making the same offer, the wording was such that it sounded almost as though acceptance was mandatory. It also ended up in the bin.

The third offer letter was delivered by hand while Andrew was at school. Ruth thought the nice man in an expensive suit was one of the solicitors. It wasn't until she had sat him down and fetched him a cup of tea and a biscuit, that she learned that he worked for the developer, and that he wasn't a very nice man at all.

Apparently, Carter Development had bought up all of the open land around her cottage. They were planning on building a small estate with just over thirty homes. Four existing homes were within the proposed estate boundary lines and would have to be razed. Three of those were under offer, subsequent to their owners having received the solicitor's offer letter.

Ruth explained that she had lived in the cottage for way too long to think of moving at her age.

The man became a little more forceful, yet remained pseudo polite. He advised her that their company could force her out under something called eminent domain.

Ruth knew perfectly well what eminent domain was, and also knew that it was only used by the government in the event that utility or county infrastructure needed the property for sanctioned improvements.

Building an estate for profit did not fit the criteria.

The man's last words, however, did trouble Ruth.

"There are other ways we can make you sell us the property. You should think very seriously about accepting the offer."

That was the last time she talked with anyone related to the project. Letters still came and her phone kept ringing, but she responded to neither. From then on, her only contact was through their acts of intimidation.

*

The first time, a brick was thrown through her window. Next, her tiny garden shed mysteriously burned to the ground.

Still, she held fast, determined to ride out the storm, as she put it. Andrew suggested she get her own solicitor, but she wouldn't hear of it. She had never trusted them. When her husband died and she was forced to use a probate solicitor, she found him aloof, pompous and was never available to answer her questions.

She hadn't spoken to a solicitor since.

Things escalated when Ruth opened her door one morning to retrieve the morning paper and found her cherished cat, Pepper, dead on her front step. One look at the poor animal's tortured body was enough to know that he hadn't passed naturally.

For a start, his head was facing the wrong way.

Andrew called the police. Ruth had been against it, but Andrew felt that things were getting too dangerous for the two of them to fight alone. He had confidence that the police could help.

The officer that answered sounded very concerned, but wasn't convinced that Pepper's death was part of an extortion plot against Ruth. He promised to send an officer over when one was free.

No officer ever came.

Two days later, while Ruth was making her way carefully down her front steps, the wooden handrail broke as she leant on it – directly at the spot that had been sawed two thirds of the way through. She fell the last few steps and landed hard on her hip.

It was broken along with her left arm.

She was admitted to Datchet Hospital. Doctors advised Andrew that she would be there for at least three weeks. She would then have to move into a convalescent home, for possibly three months or longer.

Social services immediately became involved, placing Andrew into a temporary foster facility in the centre of Reading.

It was something out of Dickens' 'Oliver Twist'. Twelve boys to a room in a Victorian building with poor heating, no hot water and food that was basically potatoes and thin, runny gravy.

Because of his small stature, he was targeted from day one by the bigger boys. The problem was that most of the occupants were bigger than Andrew. His ability to talk them out of the idea had no effect on the Reading thugs. They were much bigger and far less intelligent than those in the Inverness suburb.

He was bullied daily and that was on top of being perpetually cold and hungry.

Four weeks after Ruth's fall and one week into her stay at the convalescent home, she contracted a staph infection.

She died four days later.

When Andrew asked to attend her funeral, he was told by the facility administrator that there was no one available to accompany him to the funeral. His request was therefore denied.

*

Ruth's will left the cottage and all her other worldly possessions to The Gentle Paw cat rescue, in Twyford. Andrew was advised that he could contest the will, but he decided that Ruth should at least be permitted to have her final wishes carried out per her instructions.

Two weeks later, he noticed a news item in the 'Reading Chronicle'. Carter Development had purchased the deed for Ruth's cottage from Gentle Paw.

Being bequeathed a home was a lovely gesture by Ruth, but Gentle Paw had no idea how to market and sell the cottage. When Carter Development's solicitor called and said their client would buy it, above market in an all-cash purchase, they were ecstatic.

So was Carter Development.

*

Hilda and Walter were still standing within the tiny copse of birch trees. They hadn't been able to move in hours. They had been moments away from leaving their hide and commencing the hunt, when a dense fog suddenly blanketed the entire countryside.

They stood waiting silently for it to either burn off or at least thin enough to enable them to begin tracking their first prey.

As they stared into the grey murk, they thought they saw a slight lightening of its density. As they watched, the fog started to slowly dissipate. The dark grey became lighter and less oppressive.

The strange thing was how the heaviest layer of fog seemed to still be hugging the ground. There was a distinct line about three metres off the ground. The top layer was thinning out nicely, but the bottom part was, if anything, growing denser.

It was then that they noticed that the fog around where they were standing was also lifting. The only part that wasn't, was the dark ring that completely encircled them.

The dark perimeter started to move slowly towards them, until the grey mass was only a few metres from where they were standing.

Then, as they watched in horror, the fog rose off the

circle, and dissolved into the morning sky. The circle wasn't fog. It was made up entirely of stags. Hundreds of them. All packed together staring at the Carters.

Their snorting breath was sending clouds of condensation into the air. It looked like the entire circle was smouldering.

Hilda and Walter were initially shocked and frozen in place. Then the two started to raise their rifles.

The encircling stags charged. The copse of old-growth birch snapped like twigs.

The Carters' bones snapped like – bones.

CHAPTER
SIXTEEN

The guests were on their second Black Velvet and were feeling very festive. The fire was roaring in the grate and Christmas carols were playing gently in the background.

In the kitchen, they were in the final stages of preparing the lavish Christmas dinner. Leon had opened three bottles of an exceptionally decent claret. Helen had just put the Christmas pudding in a pot with water. It rested on an upturned plate, so it could steam slowly.

Elena was in the dining room making final tweaks to the place settings. Andrew was not exactly helping – more like messing up whatever Elena had just fixed.

"You know I still never got a believable reason as to why you moved up here – and don't give me that 'assigned here' nonsense. Being assigned to Kingussie has all the earmarks of a punishment posting. The only thing wrong with that theory is that you only just graduated. I somehow doubt that you could have upset someone in the force that soon. Come on – it's just the two of us. Why here?"

He watched her straighten a couple of glasses and refold yet another serviette.

"I told you. I like it here."

"Bullshit! You are a young guy. No way would you be happy in a tiny, one-pub town where you only get to see the sun three times a year," Elena insisted.

"What can I do to prove to you that I wanted to be here?" Andrew asked.

"Don't get me wrong. I completely believe you want to be here. It's the why that isn't working for me."

"My god, but you're pushy. Is that a Yank thing? I've seen pushy American women on TV, but always thought that was just made up."

Elena walked over and pushed him in the chest. He stepped back but she did it again.

"See! Pushy women are real," she grinned.

They both gave each other a stubborn look. Elena then smiled. "We will talk about this later."

She backed away from him and headed for the kitchen.

Andrew watched her go.

He was trying very hard to not get involved. He didn't do 'involved' very well. He knew from experience that it was far less painful being alone. Too many people whom he'd cared about had been taken from him. He wasn't sure he ever wanted that sort of pain again.

*

On an exceptionally bleak morning, three months after arriving at the Reading foster facility, he was called to the Blue Room. This was the place where the children met with prospective foster parents.

The room was sparsely furnished with cheap plastic chairs and tables. The carpet may once have been blue but was now so old and worn that it had turned a dull grey. It looked far more like a prison than a welcome centre where foster parents would meet possible candidates.

Andrew knew of the room, but this was the first time he had ever been called to make an appearance. He didn't know how he was supposed to feel. Being called to the Blue Room meant that a family had chosen to specifically meet him. They had already been vetted and were in a position to foster him. Not just foster him, but give him back some sense of purpose, rather than just be left to mentally deteriorate within the Reading facility.

Waiting for him in the room was the facility director, Hilda Hilson, and a middle-aged couple he didn't recognise. They stood to greet him. They introduced themselves as Mary and Chris Winston.

Mary looked to be a young forty, but was probably older. She was slight, with a few streaks of grey in her auburn hair. She was still pretty, with a freckled, outdoorsy complexion. Her blue eyes seemed to light up when she was introduced to Andrew.

Chris was a bull of a man. Two metres tall, barrel-chested, grey untamed hair and a smile that looked like he really meant it. He held out his hand, and gave Andrew a strong handshake while looking directly into his eyes.

"The Winstons have been wanting to foster for a while and have come here today to meet you and to see how you get along together. You should know, Andrew, that it is most unusual for a couple to request an older child," Hilda said.

"Is that what I am?" Andrew replied.

Chris Winston burst out laughing. It was an infectious laugh – rich and unabashed.

Andrew couldn't help smiling.

Hilda gestured for them all to sit. "I will leave you now. There's no time limit as such but we recommend a maximum one hour for initial meetings."

Chris looked back at her. "What if we don't need additional meetings?"

Hilda looked back at him with an air of bureaucratic superiority. "This is a very serious decision for all parties. We have found that multiple meetings are a good protocol when fostering."

Chris gave her his biggest smile. "Just out of curiosity, what is your statistical success rate on finding foster parents for children in their teens?"

Hilda became flustered and began playing with an invisible thread on her polyester jacket.

"I don't have those figures to hand, but I will do some research." She walked out of the room, at a pace that appeared to be just a tad too fast.

Chris turned to Andrew. "What an awful woman!"

They spent a little over an hour together in the Blue Room.

Chris and Mary ran an onion and leek farm just outside Wargrave. Their son, Justin, was killed by an IED just outside Basra in Iraq. It had taken them years to come to terms with the loss of their boy.

It had taken still longer for them to decide on fostering. They had no interest in raising a baby or young boy. Been there, done that. They had neither the time nor patience to go through that again. They wanted a teenager that they could mentor, and hopefully be in a position to give him or her a second chance in life.

Mary and Chris asked him hundreds of questions. Andrew ended up doing the same. It became clear that the three really wanted to know about each other. Andrew, who since his parents' death hardly ever spoke about himself, answered every question honestly then asked ones of his own.

After sixty-eight minutes, they all felt they had a pretty good idea of what made each other tick.

Mary reached across the table and took one of Andrew's hands in hers. "Do you think you would like to come and live with us?"

Andrew started crying. He hadn't cried since the day with the golden retriever. He had no advanced warning of his reaction. He just started crying. All he was able to do was nod at Mary and Chris.

Andrew moved to the onion farm two weeks later.

*

When Andrew walked out of the oppressive foster home for the last time, he felt as if a massive weight had been lifted off his soul. As the depressing facility faded in the rear-view mirror of Chris's late-model Mercedes, he felt safe for the first time in months.

Once outside the brick jungle of Reading, they were surrounded by green fields and unlimited open space. He'd forgotten what that was even like. For a brief moment it took him back to his grandmother's house. He quickly shook away that memory.

This was a new day.

Chris drove them through Sonning then Twyford, before getting on the Wargrave road. Less than a kilometre later they turned onto the farm's private drive. Andrew could immediately smell the onions. It was almost overpowering, but at the same time, reassuring. It was a familiar smell.

Their house was an extended bungalow that had originally been a small two-bedroom home. They had added two more bedrooms, a large country kitchen and a huge conservatory.

When Andrew walked in, his first sight was of a five-metre-long banner draped across the entire sitting room. It read simply –

WELCOME HOME, ANDREW

As soon as they were through the door, Mary ran over and gave Andrew the best hug he could ever remember getting. He felt his eyes starting to tear and fought hard to hold back his emotions. Then he saw that Mary was already crying. He realised that he didn't have to hold back his tears.

They first showed him his bedroom. It was amazing. It was the size of his parents' Inverness sitting room. One wall was nothing but built-in shelving. In the centre was a fifty-inch flat screen. On the shelf below was a Sky Q box and the latest PlayStation with a dozen games stacked next to it.

There was a desk with a brand-new MacBook Pro, a queen-sized memory-foam bed and an en-suite bathroom.

A built-in cabinet held new jeans, hoodies, T-shirts, undies and socks.

At the end of the 'room tour', Chris handed Andrew a brand new iPhone.

"We'll go to the Oracle at the weekend and buy you whatever else you need," Chris said.

"I don't want to spoil the celebration mood," Mary advised, "but we should also tell you that you are registered at Liggot's School. It's at the end of our drive on the other side of Wargrave Road. You're not scheduled to start till next week, so you have five days of freedom. It's a private school. We thought they'd give you a better chance of catching up, if you need to."

"I do." Andrew couldn't stop grinning.

"Anyway," Chris said. "This is your space. You do whatever you need to do to make it your own. Before you get too settled we thought we'd go into Wargrave and have lunch. Probably not as good as you're used to eating in Reading but they do a pretty good burger."

*

The Sword and Dragon gastro pub backed onto the River Thames. The restaurant was decorated in light woods, earth-tone furnishings and etched glass-table partitions. As they were seated, Andrew noticed the next table being served their order. The portions were big and it was clear that their burgers were the popular choice.

Andrew decided that it was time to confess to his new foster parents that he was a vegetarian. Chris just laughed and told him he didn't know what he was missing.

Mary, however, was intrigued. She wanted to hear more about it. She had been thinking about making their home vegetarian for a while.

That stopped Chris's laughing.

As they ate and talked over their future plans, Andrew watched as boats of every size and shape imaginable, made their way up and down stream. The image was idyllic.

So was the restaurant's black bean veggie burger and chips.

CHAPTER
SEVENTEEN

The Lodge's first Christmas dinner was served at exactly 2:00 p.m. as planned.

There had been talk of delaying the meal until Walter and Hilda bothered to show up, but that suggestion was voted down unanimously by the other four guests.

The meal was extraordinary. The geese were delicious and with Leon's superb carving, any sign of their cuts, stabbings and slashes were concealed under roasted bacon and gravy. By the time the goose, two stuffings, roasties, sprouts, cranberry and bread-sauce were plated, each dish looked like a photo definition of pure gluttony.

Despite there being enough food on each plate for a family of five, each had second helpings, and still had room for the Christmas pudding.

Once all the plates and serving dishes had been cleaned away, Elena turned off the dining room lights.

Helen appeared from the kitchen with a perfect half-dome, flaming pudding. The Adamses and the Stones applauded her entrance. She served each a large wedge of the liquor-soaked dessert. Elena then offered each person either home-made brandy butter, rum and brandy cream or just a slug of single malt, poured over the top.

They all opted for the triple whammy.

Leon then appeared, right on cue, and poured them each a glass of French dessert wine.

The Franks joined the guests for pudding and wine and made certain that the conversation was light-hearted and festive. No one even mentioned the absence of the Carters or the fact that their hosts were liberally covered with plasters on their faces and arms.

Once they were all tucking into their pudding, and sipping still more alcohol, Andrew and Elena had their Christmas dinner in the kitchen. It was the same meal, but without the goose.

Helen had also made them a vegan gravy after deglazing the previous day's roast vegetable pan with Marsala. It was delicious and was poured liberally over their veggie feast.

*

Helen had finally twigged on Christmas Eve that Andrew hadn't eaten any meat since he'd arrived. She joked with him that he was a stealth vegetarian.

*

Andrew grew to love Chris and Mary. They were perfect parents. Strict yet exceedingly fair. They both had a young outlook on life, despite their age. They were actually fun to be around. Most importantly, they were the sort of parents that didn't embarrass you when you brought friends home. There was no attempt at adopting teen interests or their lexicon. They never seemed to put on airs. They didn't need to. They were cool just the way they were.

Andrew had started school on the appointed day. He had been nervous about being accepted by his peers. Being a new boy was bad enough. Starting in the middle of term really singled you out for special attention.

His fears turned out to be unfounded. He was accepted at face value. He was a bright kid with a good sense of humour. He wasn't a threat and didn't attract attention to himself.

One thing that he never expected was that Berkshire girls had a thing about Scottish accents. His wasn't a strong one, but he had enough of a brogue to be noticeable.

Girls kept asking him to say something with a Scottish accent. He never knew quite what to say so he usually just produced a pretty good impression of Sean Connery as 007.

As none of the other students had ever heard of Connery, or seen any Bond film before Daniel Craig, they thought his little quotes were original and terribly cute.

One girl in particular captured his attention. Clare Spire was in the same form as him and therefore was in almost every class he took.

Clare was simply beautiful. She had long, naturally curly dark hair, piercing blue eyes and a fantastic laugh. The fact that she was the prettiest girl in school didn't hurt either.

She lived in the village of Charvil, about half a mile from the school. Andrew took to walking her the whole way home, despite his living almost across the street from the school.

Clare finally twigged to that fact and thankfully found it charming rather than a little stalker-ish.

They became an item just after Andrew's fourteenth birthday. On weekends, they would jump on the train in Twyford and eight minutes later be in Reading. They held hands as they strolled along the pedestrian parade of shops.

Their favourite thing to do was to wander around the Oracle shopping mall. It had everything. As neither was given a particularly large amount of pocket money, they rarely bought anything, but just being together while window-shopping seemed to be enough for both of them.

Their first kiss was in the photo booth on the lower ground floor of the Oracle. They even had a picture to prove it.

As the end of the school term approached, Andrew began counting the days to the holiday with a growing dread. The Winstons were taking him to the south of France for the entire Easter break.

They had expected him to be excited by the trip. He was, but being away from Clare for almost four weeks felt completely tragic.

They understood his angst and promised him that they could call or even Skype each other as much as they wanted. Andrew decided that that was a suitable compromise.

*

They landed at Nice Airport on a sparklingly sunny afternoon. They took a taxi to the town of Cannes, about thirty miles away. Andrew was speechless as he stared out at a whole new world. He had never been outside the UK, and hadn't somehow realised that other countries actually looked different.

The taxi drove through the outskirts of Cagnes-sur-Mer, with its rough-plastered homes and bright red tiled roofs. Even the smells were different. In the UK, no matter where you were (unless it was in the city where all you could smell was diesel), everything smelled of greenery mixed with just a touch of damp.

The south of France smelled of lavender, burning leaves, the Mediterranean and moped exhaust. Andrew found it very exotic.

The taxi cut inland then joined the autoroute that parallels the coast for the length of the Côte d'Azur. Thirty minutes later, they pulled up in front of the Hôtel du Mer, just off the Croisette.

Andrew was stunned by the Med. He was no stranger to water. As a child, he'd spent many an hour playing along the banks of the River Ness. That heavily trafficked waterway was not, however, what anyone would call beautiful. It was the arterial waterway for the industrial parts of Inverness and the surrounding towns. It was perpetually light brown unless there was an exceptionally high tide, at which point it turned a dark and murky green.

When they'd left Heathrow Airport only a few hours earlier, it had been drizzling with fog and sleet forecast for later in the day. This was something else entirely. It was late March and off season in Cannes, yet the sun was glistening off the unbearably blue waters of the Med.

People were lying out on beach loungers all geometrically

lined up in perfect harmony. Each beach had its own colour scheme and decor.

He suddenly wasn't missing Clare quite as much, though he wished she could be there with him to share in the experience.

*

They spent their days exploring. At noon, they would stop for lunch at local restaurants for a Salade Niçoise or their recommended plat du jour. Between meals, they walked for hours investigating every nook and cranny of Cannes and its surrounding villages.

Dinner was usually at a restaurant chosen by Mary. She was the food researcher of the group. Andrew was introduced to bouillabaisse, daube Provençale, ratatouille and many more local favourites. He had never eaten food like that in his life. He thought that all food was basically like English food.

At the end of their second week, Andrew got a call from Clare's father. She had been rushed to hospital. It hadn't been confirmed yet but the prognosis was that she had acute appendicitis and would require an immediate operation.

Much to Andrew's amazement, Chris, without a second's hesitation, booked two seats on the next flight out of Nice. Mary would stay in Cannes till they returned, but the boys were going to get to England before Clare even went into surgery. The fact that Chris understood how much Clare meant to him, and would mess up his own holiday to make sure Andrew could be at her side, meant the world to Andrew.

They arrived early and made it to the hospital just as Clare had been given her pre-op meds. She was feeling no pain. Her glistening, stoned eyes lit up when she saw Andrew walk into her hospital room.

The adults left them alone for a bit so they could have some privacy. Andrew kept telling her that she would be fine. She kept telling him that she really, really loved him.

The meds had clearly taken full effect.

Andrew was gently booted out of the room as the nurses readied her for the operation theatre. He joined Chris and Clare's parents in the family waiting room.

Chris and Andrew hadn't even stopped at home, so were both still in holiday clothes and were surrounded by hand luggage. The surgeon stopped by briefly to tell them about what the operation entailed. He explained that it was a very standard procedure and should be completed in less than ninety minutes. He assured them that they had nothing to worry about.

He seemed to know what he was doing and certainly had the pompous air of a surgeon. Andrew, however, couldn't help but notice that the man had oddly pointed facial features. Andrew felt he looked a little like a rodent with a superiority issue.

They sat almost wordlessly in the waiting room, watching as the wall clock ticked off one second at a time.

A surgical nurse stepped into the room just over two hours later. Everyone looked over to her to hear the good news. They realised immediately that her expression was not one of jubilation.

The nurse looked pale and very uncomfortable. She asked which was Clare's direct family.

Clare had died on the operating table. They were told it was the result of a rare surgical complication.

Clare's parents both asked to speak with the surgeon. The nurse advised that he wasn't available.

"Don't be ridiculous," Clare's father insisted. "He should have been the one to talk to us. Where is he? I want to speak with him, now!"

The poor nurse looked as if she was about to cry. "He left soon after the surgery."

"The botched surgery you mean!" he replied.

*

It took Clare's parents and their solicitor two months to find out that the rare complication that was given as the reason for her death, was that the surgeon had not properly clamped off the appendicular artery. What was worse was that he had somehow not noticed his error until there was visible loose blood in the body cavity. Clare had bled out on the operating table.

Four weeks after that, they learned that the surgeon had just been dismissed from the hospital. Clare's death was the third one in six months that was attributed to Dr Adams. Negligent malpractice was listed as the probable cause in all three deaths.

Two weeks later the local papers were filled with news of Dr Adams's arrest. It appeared that the doctor was a heavy cocaine user. It seems he had been under the influence of the drug during all three of his malpractice fatalities.

CHAPTER
EIGHTEEN

The four guests were relaxing in the lounge, warming themselves by the fire. Despite having consumed enough food and alcohol for a small wedding party, they still were managing to polish off a quick brandy before taking a well-earned nap.

Harry Stone knocked back the last sip of his drink then offered his hand to his wife, Anne.

"May I escort you upstairs, madam?"

"I'm so bloody pissed you may have to carry me," she replied.

She managed to get to her feet and together the pair weaved their way to the staircase.

"I'm heading up as well," Cynthia advised.

"You go ahead. I'll finish this off and join you in a few minutes." Douglas raised his brandy glass in a drunken toast.

Once she was gone, he stumbled to the bar and filled his brandy snifter to the top.

"I can have any fucking drink I want, when I want," he slurred.

He returned to the lounge and pulled one of the armchairs closer to the fire. He sat down heavily and stared into the roaring flames.

"I was a fucking surgeon. Nobody can tell me what to do." He gulped aggressively at the brandy.

*

Directly above him, the huge antler chandelier began to move on its own. The antler forks slowly and silently untangled themselves and straightened until the thing looked like an octopus with dozens of tentacles.

The upper forks pushed against the ceiling until it began descending while still attached by the electric cord. The tiny LED lights at the end of the antler branches started to pulsate.

The man who used to be a surgeon, but was now simply Mr Adams was oblivious. As he stared into the swirling flames, his eyes grew heavy. The chandelier continued its downward trajectory. It stopped just above Douglas's dozing head. The antlers spread slowly encircling it. The lower ones moved at lightning speed and curled around his neck.

As Douglas tried to pry it off, the entire creature twisted sharply to the right. Douglas's neck snapped with a loud 'POP'. The thing moved to the floor, snapping the electric cable. It dragged the dead body with it. Then, with horrifying speed, it ran into the fireplace and up the chimney with Douglas's lifeless body in tow.

There was a horrific sound of bones crunching and flesh rending as the thing pulled him all the way up the chimney.

All at once, a torrent of blood cascaded down onto the roaring fire, extinguishing it in a mass of pink steam.

*

No one in The Lodge heard a thing. Cynthia hadn't even made it to the bed. She was passed out cold in a large leather armchair. Had she been awake or even conscious, she might have sensed the stitching of the chair begin to loosen at the seams. The chair's arms started first. The heavy thread backed out of each sewn hole, one hole at a time.

The back of the chair was next. When all the thread had been retracted, the separate pieces of tanned hide slowly wrapped themselves around the woman.

The unsewn sections slowly started to apply pressure. Together they squeezed, tighter and tighter. Cynthia's eyes suddenly opened, but it was doubtful that she knew or saw what was happening.

The sections grew closer together as the tightening continued. Bones started to break. Then finally, parts of her body burst open under the pressure.

The sections didn't stop squeezing until Cynthia had gone from a size eighteen to a petite size 4.

There was a time when she had dreamed of being that slim.

She finally made it.

*

Andrew and his foster parents pulled up outside Ruscombe Catholic Church in the midst of a gale. The wind was bending the old oaks to an alarming angle while at the same time, whipping the willow trees into a frenetic dance.

Clare's service was conducted by the same priest who had baptised her. He told the congregation how his saddest moments were when one so young was taken.

Clare's father gave the eulogy while tears streamed down his face. His voice held a mix of devastation and anger. When he finished speaking he looked directly at Andrew.

"Would you like to say something?"

Andrew didn't know what to say. He had never contemplated standing in front of a church full of strangers and talking about Clare.

"It's the last time you'll get to speak to her directly," her father added.

He wasn't certain exactly what that meant, but almost robotically stood and made his way to the pulpit.

"Clare had a light," Andrew's voice wavered. "She could look at you and you'd feel it. Its warmth – its comfort. Clare didn't look at the world the way most of us do. She saw little things. Things that I would have never seen if she hadn't been there to show me. She saw the way a tiny flower had grown out of a solid brick, or how a beetle was walking in step to a Lady Gaga song we were listening to. Silly things undoubtedly, but things that nobody else perceived.

"Most importantly, she saw things in me that I never did. She saw my strengths and weaknesses – my fears and my dreams. She somehow saw them all.

"Now that she's gone – I can only ask, and I know I'm being selfish, but – who's going to show me all those things now?"

Andrew thought he would cry but strangely – didn't. He felt suddenly untethered from reality. He looked down at the congregation and felt as if he was watching a movie, that none of it was real. He couldn't seem to leave the pulpit. Chris walked up and put his arm around his shoulder and led him back to his seat.

The graveside service and burial was like something out of a biblical epic. As the priest started to speak, the sky turned almost black. The wind increased, sending anything not weighed down flying through the congregation. Then, the rain came. Not in drops, but in sheets. Everyone tried to protect themselves under their umbrellas, but the wind either flipped them inside out or sent them flying across the churchyard and down Ruscombe Lane.

The priest's words were lost to the storm. Rivulets of water began pouring into the empty grave. It was easy to imagine that Clare was responsible. That she was letting everyone know that she was not pleased about the outcome of her life.

Chris and Mary both had their arms around him as they made for the car once the priest gave up on the weather and ran for cover.

Andrew knew he would never forget the vision of the grave filling with water beneath the suspended casket. He hoped it wasn't their intent to lower her into that. She never learned to swim in life and was irrationally scared of water.

Andrew again became withdrawn. A darkness had pulled him into its lair. He wanted to see the light and fight back to the surface but just didn't know how to find the way.

Chris and Mary were beside themselves. Nothing they did seemed to help. They desperately wanted to help their son but didn't know how.

*

A few weeks later, the Winstons' solicitor stopped by the house. Andrew had been asked to be part of the meeting. He wasn't sure why and only had bad memories of visits by solicitors.

He assumed that his foster parents had tired of his dark mood and were going to return him to the foster home. He didn't really blame them. They hadn't signed up for whatever it was that Andrew had become.

They all sat at the dining table. The solicitor removed a folder from his briefcase then extracted a formal-looking document printed on what looked like light pink parchment.

He started to hand it to Chris but Chris gestured for it to be given to Andrew. Resigned to his fate, he took it and started to read the document. His eyes began to water. He had never seen an approved order of adoption before.

He practically dived across the table to hug his mother and father. He felt the darkness crumble around him. At least most of it. He knew though that some part of it would always be lying dormant, just below the surface.

After emotions had settled down the solicitor had one more thing to say.

"I heard yesterday something that you might find – I'm not sure interesting is the right word. Let's say enlightening."

"You've captured our interest," Chris said.

"It appears that the case against the surgeon, isn't quite as cut and dry as we thought. A company called the Dashire Group

owns the hospital where Clare died and he had privileges. It turns out that their managing director knew all about Mr Adams' drug use. He decided after the first death that the best thing to do was to sweep it under the carpet for the benefit of the stockholders. By the second instance of malpractice, he had no choice but to protect the initial cover-up. The only way he could do that was by burying the second one as well.

"The first two deaths were found to have been tragic accidents. The inquests were fast-tracked and heavily influenced by the hospital's head office."

The solicitor took a moment to give his glasses a quick wipe.

"Your persistence in having me stay on top of this has unearthed years of spotty surgical oversight by the Dashire Group, more specifically by the managing director, Harrold Stone. Mr Adams was only one of the surgeons with a highly questionable surgical mortality rate."

The three stared at him in shock.

"How could that happen?" Mary asked.

"It's not supposed to," he replied. "There's layer upon layer of oversight, but as we see all too often, if the person at the top is determined to conceal data, they usually find a way."

"So, what will happen to them?" Chris asked.

"Adams will be certain to get a substantial custodial sentence. As for Harrold Stone, I'm afraid he'll probably receive some ludicrous pay-off by the board and never spend a minute behind bars."

"Wouldn't it be wonderful if karma actually caught up with people like that?" Mary said.

Andrew looked to those seated around the table and smiled.

"Maybe one day it will."

CHAPTER
NINETEEN

Helen planned to serve a simple buffet for Christmas supper. Smoked salmon, cold lamb and chutney and a mixed salad. The guests could either have more Christmas pudding or the remains of the sherry trifle they'd had the previous day.

The only people to appear at the bar for the pre-dinner cocktails were the Stones. The Carters still weren't back from their hunt and Cynthia and Douglas Adams had put a do-not-disturb notice on their door.

Helen wanted desperately to have a word with them – as the lounge chandelier was missing and Douglas was the last person in the room that afternoon. She felt that he was just the type to get pissed enough to vandalise someone else's property. He just seemed to have that sort of nasty streak.

She would just have to wait till morning. As for the Carters – she and Leon had discussed what they should do about the missing pair. The snow had stopped, but the wind was howling at fifty knots plus. Nobody was going out in the dark to check on those idiots. They decided that the pair were simply too unpleasant to ever come to any harm and had probably by now found shelter somewhere.

*

Andrew was having a quick wash before coming down to dinner. A pounding on his door made him drop his complimentary toothbrush.

He was surprised to see Elena standing there. She looked agitated and worried. She walked in and sat on the edge of his bed.

"I don't know what to do," she stated.

"What are you talking about?"

"You know how I said that I thought that something strange was going on. Well, it is, and I can prove it."

Andrew took a deep breath and studied Elena closely.

"What's going on that's so strange?"

"People seem to be dying," she said.

Andrew chose his words carefully. "The only death I'm aware of is Alan's, and that appears to have been accidental."

Elena fidgeted with a button on her blouse. "He was only supposed to choke on the piece of meat. I just wanted to scare him."

"What are you talking about? You didn't make him choke. It just happened."

"It happened, because I made it happen." Elena looked down at her shoes.

"No, you didn't. He choked on a bone," Andrew said.

"But I wished it to happen," she insisted. "I watched him put a huge forkful of food into his mouth and I wished hard that he would choke – and he did."

"Are you telling me that you have the power to make people choke to death?" Andrew sounded incredulous.

"I must. It worked, didn't it?"

Andrew sat beside her and took her hand in his. "You wishing someone harm doesn't translate into you having killed them."

"Not even when they die?"

"Not even when they die," he replied. "Let me ask you something – have you ever wished someone harm before?"

"Of course," she said.

"And did harm come to any of them?" Andrew asked.

"Our neighbour in Maryland had a heart attack after he screamed at me when I asked him to turn his music down. I wished right then that he'd drop dead."

"How long after you wishing it did he have the heart attack?"

"About three years," she replied.

"I'm sorry to tell you, but it doesn't sound to me like you have the power of life and death. Alan just put too much food in his mouth and choked."

Elena looked up at him. "You're sure?"

"I'm sure you're not a killer."

She rested her head on his shoulder. "That's a relief."

She sat upright again, a new look of concern on her face.

"So, what did happen to Alan. Who took his body? Who butchered him?" Elena asked.

"I have no idea," Andrew replied.

"I need to show you something. I wasn't going to because you're the police and everything. I was going to go get the Franks but they seem to have something really weird going on at the moment. If I show you something will you try to not go all detective on me? I'm kinda freaked out."

Elena took Andrew's hand and led him down the hall to the Adams' room. She used her pass key to open the door. She stepped aside to let him enter.

"God, it stinks in here. Something must be... What the hell happened here?"

Elena stepped into the room and stood next to him as he stared, horrified, at what was left of Cynthia Adams. He couldn't even fathom what could have squeezed her into the elongated version of herself that lay dead on the stained plaid carpet.

There was a lot of blood and other bodily fluids on the armchair and surrounding carpet, but nothing could explain what had happened to her.

"So, you didn't do this?" Elena asked.

"No. I wouldn't even know how." Andrew gave her an amazed look. "What do you mean – did I do it? Why would you even think that?"

"I wanted to make sure it wasn't you. I mean, all this started once you arrived."

"Alan died before I got here," he stated.

"Maybe, but that's what brought you here, wasn't it?" Elena insisted.

"You really are talking a load of bollocks. You know that, don't you?"

Elena stared at him for a good few seconds, then had a thought.

"She was alone in the room – that means Mr Adams is missing."

"Unless Douglas is the one who killed her?" he suggested.

"But he's missing too."

"As are the Carters," Andrew added. "Just so we're both on the same page. We know that Alan and Mrs Adams are dead. Are we thinking that there could be three others?"

"I told you I felt something bad was happening. It's not just this." Elena gestured to the body. "Something made Mrs Adams cut her finger in the dining room. Something tripped Mr Adams on the zebra rug and something's been seriously messing with poor Leon. There's the basement thing, the tree and the fishing gear."

"I didn't know about the basement thing," Andrew said.

"I know. Leon hasn't wanted to talk about it."

They both stared for a moment at Cynthia's deformed corpse.

"What do we do now?" Elena asked.

Before he could reply, Helen screamed from somewhere outside The Lodge.

*

They ran out of the room, being careful to lock the door behind them. As they reached the downstairs hallway, they saw Leon charging by.

"Leon?" Andrew yelled. "What's happened?"

"It's Helen. She's in the shed."

Elena and Andrew followed him out of the side door. The snow had started to melt. They had to run through slush and mud to reach the outbuilding.

Helen was standing in the dressing room staring, wide-eyed at the open meat locker.

Leon grabbed her. "Are you all right? I heard you scream!"

She pointed into the locker. The three of them turned and looked.

Three more bodies had been added to the hanging meat rack. These had not been butchered cleanly like Alan.

Hilda and Walter Carter's faces were only just recognisable due to them having been battered and torn. Pieces were missing. Chunks were hanging loosely where their skin and muscle had been raked by antlers. Their bodies were hung upside down. They were still clothed though their hunting apparel was ripped and in some places shredded. The material was almost completely blood-soaked. What made it worse was that their bodies seemed shapeless. The arms, legs, torso, etc. were visible but all seemed to have no rigid form.

Andrew realised that what they were looking at were bodies where almost every bone had been either broken, or in some cases, shattered.

Douglas Adams, on the other hand, was completely naked. His skin looked to have been both burnt and scraped off. His entire body was half its normal girth but at least a third taller. He had no face. That too had been scraped off during his journey up the chimney. Though his shirt was gone – his school tie had somehow held on.

That was the only way they could recognise him.

CHAPTER
TWENTY

Andrew insisted they all leave the shed immediately. He locked the door himself, then pocketed the key. He then ushered them back through the side door and into the kitchen.

Leon was the first to speak. "What the hell is going on?"

Andrew was about to reply when Harry Stone stuck his head around the corner.

"I don't suppose you have any more of that fabulous champers, do you?"

Helen put on a brave face and retrieved a bottle from the back fridge. She handed it to him. He looked momentarily nonplussed at being handed an unopened bottle sans ice bucket.

He took it, but with a very confused look on his face. Clearly the idea of having to actually do something for oneself was foreign to the man.

Andrew waited until Harry finally wandered off with his bottle.

"Something seems to be stalking people."

"I think we all pretty much grasped that part," Leon replied. "I think the big question is, what? Four people are dead. What do we do. We can't get away…"

"Actually, it's five people," Andrew corrected. "Elena found Cynthia dead up in her room."

"Maybe we can leave," Elena interrupted. "The snow's been melting all day. The road might be clear enough so that we could drive out."

They all looked at her in wonder. None of them had had that thought. It was way too obvious.

"Right," Leon said. "Grab whatever you need, then let's get as far away from this place as possible!"

"What about Mr and Mrs Stone?" Elena added.

"They're the only guests still alive. If we want that Yelp review it might be a good idea to tell them what's going on. They can't give us a rating if they're dead." Helen's tone dripped with alcohol-fuelled sarcasm.

"I'll tell them." Leon took charge. "Helen, grab whatever you need. Andrew, all the car keys are on a hook by the front door. The guest names are on them. The Stones' will take their own car obviously. Find one for us. Elena, lock all the doors and windows. We'll all meet outside in five minutes."

Nobody hesitated. Andrew grabbed all the keys except the Stones' then stepped out into the freezing night. He immediately realised that the temperature had to be below freezing and dashed back inside to retrieve the spare anorak.

Once outside again, he checked the keys and chose one of the BMW fobs. He felt they might as well escape in one of the better built cars. The name tag showed that it had belonged to the Adamses. They clearly would have no need for it any more.

He pressed the unlock button on the fob, and a dark coloured BMW 6-series flashed its headlights as the doors unlocked. He jumped inside and pushed the starter button.

The engine turned over but didn't start. Suddenly Andrew smelled petrol. Lots of it. He then felt something at his feet.

It was the rats. The foot well was filling up with them. They were crawling in from the engine compartment. They'd obviously chewed through the hoses as they'd done on the Nissan.

Andrew threw himself out of the car, kicking a couple of rats off his shoes and trousers.

The front door of The Lodge flew open and the Stones came charging out. They carried nothing. The moment they were told what was going on, they just ran.

Before Andrew could stop them, they jumped into the Vauxhall and turned the key. It didn't start. Andrew could see petrol being pumped out onto the snow from somewhere under the bonnet.

Andrew screamed at them to get out. By the light of The Lodge's Christmas decorations, he saw rats climbing up Anne's shoulders. She was screaming. Her voice was greatly muffled within the sealed car. Harry looked over at her and saw that the rodents were at her face.

Harry turned the ignition key again.

A spark flashed under the car followed by a low 'frump'. The next second, the car exploded. It lifted straight upwards, somehow remaining perfectly horizontal. It crashed back down as the flames engulfed the entire vehicle. Even in the dark, Andrew could make out hundreds of little black bodies scattering in every direction. He staggered back to The Lodge entrance.

As he watched in shocked amazement, the flames found the trail of fuel from the BMW he'd tried to start.

Its detonation was nowhere near as graceful as the Vauxhall. It simply exploded in all directions sending burning parts high into the air.

"So, we're not driving then?" Helen stated.

Andrew turned and saw that the others had joined him on the front landing.

"I wouldn't," Andrew said.

Leon took in the whole scene. "I say we walk. At least we won't be trapped inside."

The consensus was immediate. They started down the narrow drive towards the road. The snow that had previously melted during the day to a slushy mix, was now starting to freeze over as the night temperature took effect.

Their steps made loud crunching sounds in the otherwise silent night. The Christmas decoration gave them some illumination, the burning wrecks, even more. Even that diminished, however, with each step they took further away from The Lodge.

"What's that?" Helen asked pointing to where their drive joined up with the road. Dark shapes stretched out on either side for as far as they could see. There was no definition or movement. Just motionless shapes.

Leon produced a high-power LED torch from his coat pocket. He pointed it at them and turned it on.

By the harsh beam of the torch, they could see that the shapes were actually stags. Hundreds of them. They stood side by side encircling the entire property line. Steam plumed from their flaring nostrils.

Helen gasped. "This isn't happening."

The four took a step backwards. That small motion seemed enough to animate the living barrier. The stags moved as one cohesive unit. With military-like precision, the stags started to march towards them.

Without discussion or forethought, the four turned and ran as fast as they could back to the relative safety of The Lodge. Once they were in full motion, the stags stopped their approach and again stood still.

They resumed their vigil.

*

Once back inside, they locked the front door, then, as if by instinct, headed straight for the bar. Leon grabbed the first bottle he saw and poured four sizeable drinks.

There was no toasting or tasting. These were medicinal. All four downed their glasses in one.

Helen looked about to snap. "Will somebody please tell me what the hell is happening?"

Leon refilled the glasses.

"I think it may be me," Andrew announced.

Helen stared at him as if he'd suddenly spoken Aramaic.

"I won't bore you with the whole saga but when my parents were killed, I was alone beside what was left of their car. I was surrounded by dead and dying animals who'd been in the transport vehicle. There was an energy to their death. A force. Their screaming, their pain, it passed into me. I don't know how else to describe it."

The Franks both stared at Andrew as if hoping he would start making some sense.

"I always felt after that day that some – residue of that force was still inside me."

"Are you trying to tell us that you are controlling the animals?" Leon asked.

"No, not at all, but I think I'm the reason they are doing what they're doing."

"What a load of crap," Leon blurted out.

"Your guests were here for this holiday because of me," Andrew explained. "I made sure that they would all be here. They thought that they had won the trip as part of a drawing. Each believed it was a publicity stunt to do with the launch of a new electric car. Not only did they think they'd won the holiday but they thought they would each be receiving one of the new cars before they returned home. They were all told that the prize had one condition. That they never discussed it with the other guests."

"But why…?" Helen asked.

"Because all of them – that's not true – I should say all of the men, were responsible for things that happened to me growing up. Walter Carter was responsible for the death of my grandmother, Douglas Adams, the death of my girlfriend and Harry Stone tried to protect Mr Adams and let him continue practising surgery until he killed Clare."

"But what about Alan? He didn't do anything to you," Elena said.

"Not directly, but before he became a fanatic ornithologist, he was the general manager of an animal transport company. The driver who killed my parents worked for Alan. He was on his third shift in a row. He apparently needed the money and Alan didn't see any harm in bending the rules a little. The man was asleep at the wheel when he lost control. He hadn't slept in over thirty-six hours."

"You said you had nothing to do with his death." Elena looked furious.

"I didn't think I did. I came up here to scare the hell out of them and maybe cause a few accidents. That's it. I wasn't even here when Alan died. But, I think the power of my hatred for those people somehow caused all this."

"But why were their wives killed?" Leon asked, trying to sound rational.

"That's the thing," Andrew continued. "The power that I felt from the dying animals that day – was intense. I think some of that power transferred over to me. It's not as if I can use it or do anything with it, but I think just by my having it and being within a proximity to certain places, it can somehow empower the animals."

"Oh, come on." Leon wasn't buying it. "Why would a bunch of animals suddenly feel the need to slaughter a hotel full of guests because you've empowered them?"

"This place that you've created – your lodge – it has one purpose. To bring people together so they might slaughter animals. You wonder why they might want to take some sort of primitive revenge on the people who've been killing them? I am amazed they haven't done so before."

"Um…" Elena tried to find the words. "I think they might have. You know the people that sold all the hunting memorabilia on eBay?"

The Franks both nodded.

"They were selling everything on behalf of their deceased daughter and son-in-law."

"What's that got to do with anything?" Leon demanded.

"They were the owners of a hunting-themed hotel. They offered hunting packages. Their selling pitch was that you could kill it in the morning then eat it that same night."

"And?" Helen asked.

"Seven people died, including the owners," Elena said. "The police still don't know who did it, but…"

"This is absurd," Leon stated.

"Something's killing everyone," Helen voiced. "Those stags outside are certainly acting strangely."

"Did the hotel have a meat locker?" Andrew asked.

"Among other things," Elena replied.

"Jesus!" Helen took a huge gulp of her drink.

"So, what does all this mean?" Leon asked. "All the animals are out to reap vengeance on hunters? That's about ten percent of the whole country."

"I think it's more targeted than that," Andrew said.

"How?" Leon asked. "What could some hotel in…"

"Newton-on-Ouse," Elena finished for him.

"What could some hotel in Newton-on-Ouse have in common with us, other than the hunting?"

Three pairs of eyes turned to Andrew.

"I may have been there once. A group of us were on field training before our final police exam and ended up in the village at the end of one of the days' training exercises. We went to the Safari Inn for a quick sandwich and a drink."

"Safari Inn?" Helen said. "Really!"

Leon shushed her then turned back to Andrew. "Go on."

"There's not much more to say. We ate – had a drink, then we left. That was it."

"But that wasn't it, was it?" Elena asked.

Andrew took a moment to organise his thoughts.

"When we were there, I saw all the memorabilia. The stuffed animals, the stag heads, all of it. I remember feeling angry about so much pointless killing. The angrier I became, the more I felt that force from the night by the motorway."

"So, what did you do?" Leon asked.

"Nothing. Absolutely nothing. We finished our drinks and left. We heard about the incident afterwards, during my exams. I didn't realise back then that I was the catalyst. I only found that out over the last few days."

"Aren't we lucky?!" Helen was slurring her words. The alcohol was taking effect.

"If you think all this is because of you – isn't there some way you can stop it?" Leon asked.

"I don't think so. They're being driven by one thing."

Leon gave him a questioning look.

"They are being driven to kill the meaters," Andrew stated.

"Meters?" Helen asked.

"Meat eaters. They can sense who has recently eaten their flesh – their blood. I think it's also possible that they can sense who has killed recently."

"Oh, come on!" Leon said.

"There was one survivor at the Safari Inn. The housekeeper. She wasn't harmed," Andrew said.

"Why?" Leon looked unconvinced.

"She was a vegetarian. Never ate meat or fish."

"That actually makes some sense," Elena said. "The first person to die was Alan. He killed the quail for the first dinner. He was the first to be killed. Hilda and Walter shot the deer on Christmas Eve and we can assume they were the next to die."

"Oh fuck," Helen slurred.

"What are we supposed to do? Just sit here and wait for something to get us?" Leon said. "Wait a minute. All the things that have been happening to us – are you saying they are all part of this? The basement, the tree? But how? I mean let's assume that we aren't all hallucinating this – and we accept that the animals are empowered somehow. What about the dead things? What about the bloody angel? How could the angel attack me?"

"I had a look at it when we were tidying up. Did you know that it was made of carved ivory?" Andrew asked.

"No, I didn't." Leon hung his head. "So even long-dead parts of animals are dangerous now?"

"I believe they still hold some essence of life. Like DNA in an old hair follicle," Andrew suggested.

"Even the rug?" Helen sounded horrified at the thought.

All three turned and looked into the lounge. The zebra lay motionless on the wood floor. They each took a gulp of their drinks.

"Things seem calm at the moment," Andrew said. "We just have to make sure to stay together. My people should be here soon. They know where I went and that I haven't checked in."

"I hope you're right, son," Leon replied. "Let's just hope things remain quiet till your crew gets here."

The radiator suddenly started banging and clanking. The one in the lounge followed suit. Within moments all of the radiators within The Lodge began shaking violently.

Everyone turned to Andrew as if he could explain what was happening.

Then the lights went out.

CHAPTER
TWENTY-ONE

The darkness was cloyingly impenetrable. It was complete. There was no glimmer of illumination anywhere. The blackness almost felt alive. It was an entity. Albeit a negative one.

The banging and grinding sounds from the radiators increased in both intensity and volume.

They could hear Leon start to hyperventilate. It sounded like he couldn't breathe. He was gasping for air.

Andrew felt his way to him then patted down his coat pockets. He found the torch. He turned it on.

One of the large mounted antler trophies was on Leon's back. The forks had curled around his neck and were tightening. Leon was turning blue.

Andrew tried to pull the thing off by the polished wood mounting plaque, but that just made the forks tighten. They were no longer hard, bony appendages. They were alive, flexible and had lengthened.

Andrew couldn't help thinking that the thing looked very similar to the creature that exploded out of the egg in Ridley Scott's movie, *Alien*.

Andrew spotted a battery-powered firelighter behind the bar. He lit it and held it under one of the tentacles.

The creature began thrashing its other forks, trying to grab Andrew. He managed to keep them away while still holding the flame in place.

The thing suddenly released its grip on Leon's neck, fell to the ground and scurried away.

Andrew grabbed Leon before he collapsed to the floor.

He leant him against the bar then shined the torch out into the hallway and the lounge.

The beam of light looked almost solid as it cut through the utter blackness.

Stag heads, antler racks, antler wall sconces, all scurried to get out of the light. As he watched in paralysing horror, the zebra skin rug started to rise from the floor. It began to reform back into its natural living shape or as close as possible considering all the missing parts.

The others joined Andrew, watching as it started to walk towards them.

"That's it!" Helen announced. "I'm getting a gun."

Before they could stop her she dashed across the hallway and through the kitchen. The battery-operated emergency socket lights began to finally flicker on, offering a weak, yet badly needed glow. She got to the storage room and tried to open their private gun locker. It was locked. She swore to herself then produced her household keys from her pocket.

She fumbled crazily to find the right one. The industrial freezer next to the gun locker started to slowly rock back and forth. She found the key and finally got it into the hole.

She flung open the locker door as the freezer lid began opening on its own.

Helen grabbed one of the shotguns and a handful of shells and began loading it. The freezer lid flipped open the rest of the way. Helen was trying not to look. She kept her focus on loading the shotgun.

A shadowy figure began rising from the depths of the freezer. Helen finally had to look, but couldn't make out what she was looking at. It wasn't until it was fully upright that she could see detail.

Almost like a fictional Golam forming from inanimate dirt and mud, this creature had formed from the contents of the meat and fish in the freezer.

Its form wasn't human or animal. It was just a rising mound of food parts. She could make out bacon and sausages from the breakfast buffet. Frozen steaks, lamb chops, chickens, pork ribs, even the kippers had melded into the creature.

She watched in rapt horror as it grew out of the freezer and folded itself over the front edge and oozed onto the floor. She saw with revulsion that the top of the Golem thing seemed to be evolving into some sort of misshapen head. What was worse was that it seemed to be looking at her.

The eyes were just an illusion formed from the animal parts but still, they definitely looked like they were watching her.

Then it started to move towards her. She could see by the dim glow of the emergency lights that it was leaving a trail on the floor. She at first thought it could be blood, then realised that it looked to be gravy.

"That's enough," she said to herself.

She pointed the double-barrelled gun at the centre mass of the thing and pulled both triggers.

The creature splattered against the open lid and wall behind. Meat and fish parts went everywhere. Helen felt a momentary relief until she saw that the parts seemed to be reforming. Pieces of blown apart steak sought out other scattered chunks and joined together.

She ran out of the storage room and collided with the other three who were running to see what had happened.

"The loft!" Elena exclaimed. "There's no animal stuff up there. We can lock ourselves in."

"Lead the way," Leon voiced croakily.

Helen first reloaded the shotgun then followed Elena up the stairs.

Andrew ran ahead to the next floor to check if it was clear. Leon was still having trouble catching his breath and was only halfway up. He kept having to stop and force as much air into his lungs as he could manage.

The sound of frantic scurrying from the hallway below made Andrew stop. He pointed the torch down the stairs.

The hallway was now filled with all of the animal memorabilia. At the front of the group near the stairs were the taxidermic creatures from the basement. They were looking right back up at him.

He tried to get up a few more stairs without alerting them. It didn't work. The entire menagerie suddenly charged at Leon. The first to reach him was the fox. It dug its teeth into his ankle and pulled.

Leon lost his balance and slid down a couple of stairs. Elena screamed from the top step but it was too late. The stuffed creatures dragged Leon down to the hallway with frightening speed.

Once there, the entire ensemble circled him. Leon wanted to cry out but at the same time didn't want to agitate them. He still hoped that some way out would materialise.

Elena and Helen stood on the top step screaming for the animals to back off. Helen wanted to shoot the damn things but couldn't guarantee a clean shot that wouldn't also hit Leon. Andrew ran back to them from the landing of the floor above.

"What are they doing?" he asked.

"They're just watching him," Helen replied. "I don't want to do anything to make them attack him."

"What if I go down?" Andrew suggested. "They shouldn't attack me."

"You don't know that for a fact and our strength is in our numbers," Helen replied. "Let's just see what happens. They have stopped attacking him. That's a good thing."

The circle around Leon remained intact as if they were waiting for something. From the back of the hallway, the ginger cat appeared. The circle parted to let it through. It walked awkwardly over to Leon. It sniffed at him a few times then slowly pushed its face across his shoulder. This normally cute display of affection was horrific in the current surroundings. The cat repeated the push then moved down to Leon's legs then his ankle. The cat looked at the bleeding wound where the fox had bitten him.

The cat rubbed his face in the blood. It began to purr, then walked over to the fox. It slowly rubbed its face across the fox's snout leaving a smear of Leon's blood.

The others watched from the top of the stairs as the fox was officially bloodied.

The cat then stepped out of the circle.

Before Andrew and the others could react, the creatures all attacked Leon at once. They bit, ripped and clawed. The fox was given the prize piece of him. It stepped quickly onto Leon's stomach and in one savage move, sank his teeth into Leon's neck then pulled his head back, severing both carotid arteries. A momentary fountain of blood rose in the air then descended back down onto the upturned faces of the animals.

Helen screamed.

The others had to hold her back.

The entire animal gathering then slowly turned their attention to the people on the stairs. Their blood-soaked faces looked up at them. Their lifeless eyes stared at them.

The animals abandoned Leon and started to march up the stairs. Helen took one shot at them, but even though many were hit with pellets – it didn't even slow them down.

Andrew pushed the others off the landing and down the guest-room hallway to the loft stairs. They bolted the door behind them and ran the rest of the way up to the loft.

CHAPTER
TWENTY-TWO

The converted loft space was smaller than Andrew expected. There was a narrow hallway with one door on either side. Helen led them into the one on the right.

The flat had a tiny but cosy sitting room, a kitchenette, a good-sized bedroom and an en-suite. The sitting room had a sofa against one wall, a faux Chinese cabinet against another with a flat screen TV on top of it. In the far corner was an antique world globe mounted on a brass pedestal.

Helen collapsed onto the sofa and buried her head in her hands. She cried and screamed at the same time. There was a mix of loss, fear and hopelessness.

Elena sat beside her and put her arm around her.

Andrew checked out the flat's windows and its door to work out how best to barricade them in. The windows were new and triple glazed, so it was unlikely anything could come in that way. There were no skylights and no fireplaces. He felt they were pretty secure.

A few wall socket emergency lights were on, but were dimming as their batteries began to run low.

He went into the kitchenette and found some mugs, builder's tea and a kettle.

Andrew made the teas, then brought them back to the others. They drank in silence.

"The police should be here at first light," Andrew said. "We only have to hold on till then. We should be safe in here."

"I need to get something from my room. It's the door across the hall. It'll only take a second," Elena mentioned almost nervously.

"Is it essential?"

"I think so," she replied. "I want to get my passport and work permit. I might not be able to get them later, and the police will want to see them."

"I think the police will be interested in much bigger things than your residency," Andrew commented.

The radiator gave a sudden lurch followed by a deeper grinding noise.

"That can't be good," Helen mumbled.

"Please, Andrew. I really want my passport."

"I'll have to go with you. Helen – lock the door behind us. We'll be less than a minute. There's no other way in here. You'll be fine."

Helen waved them off.

Andrew listened at the door to make sure the hallway was clear. He then opened it and stepped out with Elena only centimetres behind. He quickly shut the door and waited to hear Helen lock it behind them. After a few moments, she hadn't locked it, so he poked his head back into the flat.

"Helen. It's vital you lock this door."

She appeared from the sitting room looking none too stable. Andrew backed out of the door and this time heard the lock engage.

Andrew crossed the hall to Elena's door. He put his ear against the wood and listened for any sounds. He heard nothing but the sound of the wind outside.

Elena opened her door. The first thing they saw was that her bedroom window was wide open. The second, was a huge raven standing on her chest of drawers, staring as the two slowly entered the room. Elena tried to approach the drawer where she kept her documents, but the bird raked a claw along her wrist, drawing blood.

As if to show its dominance, the bird spread its wings and let out a deafening 'cacaw'.

Elena backed up to the door, trying to work out how to best get the raven away from the drawers.

*

Helen lay down on the sofa and closed her eyes. She felt completely numb. When she had woken up this morning, she wouldn't have believed it possible that she would later watch her husband die a horrific death. It was too inconceivable to be real. She tried to force herself to believe it was all a dreadful nightmare, however the emergency lights and the banging radiators re-enforced the reality of the situation. She was slowly going into shock.

She closed her eyes to try and ward off the images she had just witnessed.

*

Andrew saw that Elena's robe was on the back of the door. He grabbed it and slowly approached the bird. He held the robe like a fishing net and tried to cast it over the top of the raven. He wasn't even close. It fell to the floor to the left of the chest of drawers. The raven just looked at it with a complete lack of interest.

He tried to manoeuvre himself closer and snag the robe by his foot. The moment he got anywhere close, the bird hopped to the edge of the cabinet and screeched threateningly, while swinging his talons in the air above the robe.

*

Helen was asleep. Across the room from her was a brightly painted, recently plastered wall. Behind that was the chimney breast from the downstairs fireplace in the lounge. Elena's parents had had it plastered over to make the room look a little more modern.

Had Helen been awake, she would have heard a scraping sound coming from the wall. She might even have seen a tiny flake of plaster fall from it, exposing the bricks beyond.

*

Elena had straightened a coat-hanger that was also behind the door and was trying to poke the raven into moving, or better still, leaving altogether.

The giant bird managed to grab the end of the wire hanger and pull it out of Elena's hand.

Elena was furious.

Andrew tried to crawl on his hands and knees to grab the robe and hanger. The raven spread his wings menacingly, and looked about to dive onto Andrew's back.

Elena had had enough. She took two steps then threw herself at the startled bird. She tackled it around its middle and together the two slid across the top of the chest of drawers and landed in a heap on the other side.

The raven went berserk. It tried to claw at Elena with its talons but was facing downwards and couldn't get its legs in an attack position.

Andrew grabbed the robe and as Elena moved aside, he wrapped it around the bird. He stepped to the window and threw the robe and bird out into the darkness. He immediately slammed the window shut.

"That was my favourite robe!" Elena joked.

*

Helen was now sound asleep and emitting a gentle snore. A jagged circle of plaster, almost half a metre wide had fallen off the wall opposite the sofa. Three bricks lay on the floor as something on the other side continued to scrape away at the mortar.

*

Elena rifled through her drawer and found the documents. They turned to leave.

"Wait. My grandmother's ring!"

She opened the bottom drawer and found a faded red velvet ring box. She checked that the ring was still inside then joined Andrew at the door.

He checked the hallway. It was clear. They quickly moved to the other door and gently knocked.

There was no reply.

They knocked louder.

Still nothing.

Andrew put his ear to the door and heard what sounded like something cracking, followed by a scuttling noise. He took a step back and kicked in the door.

They rushed in and froze in horror.

The missing antler chandelier from the lounge was dragging Helen across the floor to a ragged opening in the wall. It was obvious that she was already dead by the way her head was hanging to the side at an impossible angle.

Andrew took a step towards the thing. It moved with supernatural speed and dived into the hole while still clutching Helen by the neck. Before Andrew could do anything, they vanished into the wall.

They could hear them moving up the plastered-over chimney. They also heard Helen's bones breaking as she was dragged up the chimney.

CHAPTER
TWENTY-THREE

Andrew and Elena tried to plug and cover up the hole with anything they could find. Neither doubted that whatever had taken Helen could easily find its way back for them, but they felt that they had to do something.

Tears flowed down Elena's face as she forced blankets tightly into the old chimney breast. Andrew then dragged the sofa across the room to wedge against the hole when Elena was done.

They suddenly heard a sound from outside. Andrew ran to the window and saw red and blue flashing police lights way off in the distance. Their sirens were almost a whisper carried upon the wind.

"They're here. Look." He pointed them out to Elena. "We have to get downstairs."

"How the hell are we going to do that?" Elena sounded frantic.

Andrew started to open the dormer window. Black shadows descended from every direction and alighted on the sharply sloping roof.

Ravens. Hundreds of them stood along the guttering encircling the entire roof. They silently watched Andrew as he reclosed the window.

Andrew's brain began running escape scenarios. None seemed viable. A devious smile crossed his lips.

"Do they have any alcohol up here?"

"I'm sure they do – did. They must have had the occasional nip when they were alone."

"Let's find it," he said excitedly.

They started in the kitchenette. All they could find were the dregs at the bottom of a bottle of cooking sherry. They focussed on the sitting room.

They ripped open a black lacquered cabinet and found glasses and books, but no booze.

They lifted the lid on the coffee table and found DVDs, a laptop and car magazines.

They turned their attention to the bedroom. They tore the place apart. They couldn't find a drop. They even inspected every corner of the bathroom but without success.

They returned to the sitting room, despondent and frustrated. Andrew's brainstorm was a pipe dream without alcohol. He stared at the expensive-looking globe and wondered. He stepped over to it and rubbed his hand across its smooth surface.

"What the hell are you doing?" Elena asked.

Andrew moved his hand over the back side of the globe and felt a clasp. He flipped it up, then lifted one end. The globe swung open on a hinge. The entire top half revolved into the base to reveal a very well-stocked bar.

"I'm about to save our lives," he answered, relieved.

He started checking out the various bottles as he looked for the ones with the highest alcohol content. He found a good selection. It seemed the Franks had more than a little nip when alone up in their flat.

They carried the six that Andrew selected into the kitchenette and emptied each to the halfway mark.

Andrew ran into the bedroom and grabbed some of Leon's T-shirts from the chest of drawers.

He grabbed one last bottle from the globe and joined Elena in the kitchenette. He showed her how to make Molotov cocktails, praying that they'd work having only seen it done in movies.

"What's the seventh bottle for?" she asked.

He removed the silver topper and took a large glug. "It's for us."

He handed her the bottle and she followed his lead.

Andrew tore Leon's shirts into strips. He then stuffed them into the six prepped bottles.

Andrew shook each one repeatedly to saturate the cloth. Elena produced a plastic shopping bag for wine purchases. It had six divided sections. He could use one for each bomb.

Elena grabbed the shotgun from the other room, then had a thought.

"We don't have any spare shotgun shells. They were all in Helen's pockets."

"Then we'd better make the two cartridges that are in the gun count," Andrew stated. "We need a lighter. I left the one we had on the bar downstairs."

"Will matches do?" she asked. "I saw some in the bathroom next to a scented candle."

"Perfect!"

Elena ran off to get them. Andrew closed his eyes and worked out the order of events that had to take place to give them any chance of getting away.

When Elena returned he described what she needed to do once they were at the top of the main stairs. Timing was going to be everything.

Andrew checked the window to see if the police vehicles were close. They were, but not close enough. They had pulled up short of the drive. The cordon of stags was still there. There was no way for the police to get around them. The strobing police lights illuminated the creatures who stood unmoving in front of them. He could see officers trying to push them along but they weren't budging.

Andrew wondered if they'd be stupid enough to try driving though the animal stockade. He hoped they wouldn't. He somehow knew that wouldn't end well. He thought of shouting, but the crows were still on the roof and if anything, their numbers had increased.

"I just had a thought," Elena said. "They might not want to attack us. They've killed everyone who had eaten or harmed animals. They might leave us alone and let us walk out."

Andrew looked doubtful. "Maybe, but there's no rule book for what's going on. Besides…"

"Besides what?"

"Nothing, I'm just being paranoid," Andrew said.

"Just because you're paranoid, doesn't mean people aren't after you."

"What?" Andrew gave her a troubled look.

"It's an old joke. Forget it. Sorry I spoke."

There was an uncomfortable silence as Andrew placed each bottle in the wine carrier. He forced a smile for her benefit.

"You ready?" asked Andrew.

"As much as I'll ever be," she replied.

They made their way to the flat's entry door. It wasn't completely closed after being kicked in. Andrew peered through a large crack, then listened intently.

He could neither hear nor see a thing other than the trembling radiators. They sounded as if they were vibrating. The effect was like one constant discordant note.

He tried to open the door quietly but after having been smashed in a few minutes earlier, it screeched on its hinges and dragged on the carpet.

They left the relative safety of the flat, and slowly walked down the short hallway to the loft stair door. The light in the hall was negligible. The battery back-up lights were almost completely drained of power. Andrew held the bottle bag in one hand and the matches in the other. Elena was trying to shine the torch where needed, while also keeping the shotgun in a ready position.

Andrew flipped the lock and opened the door a fraction. He did a quick check through the gap and again saw no sign of the creatures.

They walked down the stairs, armed and ready. The only light came from the torch. Halfway down, Andrew stopped again and the two listened for any unwelcome sounds. There was nothing from the animals, but there was a strange throbbing sound coming from below. They could also hear the downstairs radiators. They were no longer just vibrating – they sounded like they were about to shake themselves off their mounts.

They made it to the guest-room hallway and saw that the emergency light had failed entirely. The torch was their only light source and it was beginning to flicker. There was no sign of the animals so they walked as quietly as possible towards the main staircase.

As they were passing the Adams's room, they saw that the door was wide open. They heard a wet slurping sound from within. Elena pointed the torch into the room.

Cynthia's body was in the centre of the room. Two enormous crows were sitting on her unmoving chest, dining on pieces of her face. Both stopped their feast and stared at the source of the torchlight.

Their beaks were red with blood. One had a strand of flesh hanging from its maw.

Elena turned the light away and looked like she was about to gag.

"Try not to," Andrew whispered.

She nodded her understanding.

They walked past the open room and were almost at the landing when their torch died completely. Andrew's first thought was despair until he saw a warm orange light coming up from the main staircase.

They approached the landing with a mix of utter fear and curiosity. Once at the top of the staircase they could see the light source.

All of the antler racks that had been converted into lamps and sconces were positioned down one side of the stairs. Their antler tips were illuminated. The light they provided gave the stairs and hall below a golden hue.

At the bottom of the stairs they could clearly see the creatures – every one of them. They filled the entire hallway except at the base of the stairs. There they had left a one-metre-wide pathway that led from the last step to the entry lobby and front door.

None of the animals looked to be in attack mode. They were still. Their faces impassive. Their eyes however were fully focussed on Andrew and Elena.

"They look as though they're letting us leave," Elena whispered. "Shall we keep going?"

"Not much choice. Just be ready."

The pair moved down one stair at a time, stopping to gauge the vibe from the hallway below with each step. Though still being watched, Andrew and Elena could see no sign of an imminent attack.

They made it to the last step. The gap between the creatures was still there. The throbbing sound was much louder on the ground level. Andrew could tell it was coming from below. From the basement. Judging by the metallic twang that went with the throbbing, he was pretty sure it was the boiler.

They both took the biggest step – the one onto the hallway floor – together.

They walked the narrow path between the animals. They could smell the rot and mildew coming from them. There was also a distinct coppery smell that could have only come from blood. Still, they remained completely stationary, and let them pass without aggression.

Andrew and Elena reached the front door.

Andrew was still not convinced that they were being allowed to leave.

"Let me go first. We don't know what they have waiting for us outside."

Elena nodded and took a firmer hold on the shotgun. Andrew removed one of the Molotov cocktails and lit the soaked cloth.

He then opened the door and stepped out. He quickly looked in all directions including straight up, but saw nothing. He pulled the cloth out of the bottle and stamped it out on the ground.

"I think we're okay." He smiled back at Elena just as the heavy door slammed shut trapping her inside the house.

Andrew could see her through the door's semi-circle glass window insert. She looked terrified. She banged at the glass but it wouldn't break.

Andrew screamed at the door. "Use the gun!"

She couldn't hear. He mimed it. That did the trick. She pointed it at the top half of the door and, once Andrew had stepped back, pulled the trigger.

The safety glass dissolved in a shower of diamond-like particles. Andrew ran back to the door. The window had been set into the top half of the door. They could now see each other clearly, but the half circle was way too small for her to crawl through.

"Why?" she screamed. "They let you out. Why not me? I'm a vegan, for Christ's sake."

"I don't know," he shouted back.

"Yes, you do." She started crying. She looked to him for the answer.

"It was the pies," he stated.

"What!?"

"The mince pies you ate, remember? Leon used the original recipe."

"So what?" she screamed.

"The original recipe used mince – actual mincemeat!"

"What does that even mean?"

"He used real minced beef. You ate beef."

She stared at him through the half circle with a look of utter confusion.

"They know what you ate," Andrew shouted.

"But you let me," she pleaded.

"I didn't think any of this was going to happen. You were enjoying it so much I didn't want to say anything."

"You knew I was a vegan. You let me eat meat without knowing."

"I didn't want to upset you," he explained.

"Well I am fucking upset now."

He was about to say something else when he saw two shadows appear behind Elena. As they grew nearer he recognised the fawn and the doe that Walter Carter had killed. They were walking on their hind legs. Their lifeless bodies seemed stretched from their time in the locker. Their heads were misshapen from the force of the bullets.

They stood behind Elena and for a brief moment looked over at Andrew. Andrew screamed at them to stop but they paid him no heed.

The two deer used their front legs to encircle Elena and pull her away from the door and into the hallway. As Andrew watched, the gap between the animals at the bottom of the stairs closed as the other creatures all approached Elena.

She looked once back at Andrew. Her face showed fear and resignation.

All the antler lights suddenly went off. Andrew was looking at complete darkness inside the house.

He heard her scream just once.

As he tried to see through the blackness, he saw a jet of yellow flame burst out of the basement doorway in the wet room. The entire lodge trembled. He knew he should move but couldn't.

Multiple burly arms grabbed him and pulled him down the front steps. Andrew struggled against them.

"There, there, lad. Calm down. We've got you."

Andrew then saw that a number of uniformed officers were trying to get him clear of the building.

"But she's inside," he yelled. "We have to…"

The Lodge exploded.

The force of the blast knocked Andrew and the other officers off their feet. Andrew managed to sit up and look back at the old manor farm.

The force of the blast had blown out the entire ground floor, causing the two upper floors to collapse upon it. Flames were pouring out of every window, door and opening, as if they too were trying to escape.

Andrew stared at the remains of the building as it burned itself to the ground. One last explosion sent sparks and debris high up into the night sky.

Suddenly, a round, fuzzy ball hit him in the chest and rolled down to his lap. It was smoking.

Andrew looked down. The fuzzy ball was the head of the stuffed ginger cat.

It was looking right at him.

Even with its burned fur and charred features, Andrew could tell that it was smiling.

Andrew started to scream.

EPILOGUE

The Firelight Inn looked like a bejewelled crown, nestled halfway up Flat Iron Mountain. The inn was only a few miles above the scenic town of Glenwood Springs. Built over a hundred and fifty years earlier, it was a landmark in that part of Colorado. Despite its gloried history and continued popularity, it had always had one drawback.

When a big enough snowstorm came in across the Rockies, they were completely cut off. The narrow mountain road became impassable after only a foot of snow. The main access was via a breathtaking aerial tramway that had been built in the sixties to take some of the strain off the tiny access road. It could keep running if it was snowing so long as the wind stayed under twenty knots.

It was the night before Thanksgiving and the inn was full to capacity. All ninety-two rooms and suites had been booked. It was their annual tradition to offer a spectacular high-altitude Thanksgiving package that included both a wild turkey and deer hunt. They were always sold out, years in advance.

This year looked like it was going to get interesting. A storm system off the coast of California had suddenly decided to head east. It was due to hit the Rockies starting around 9:00 p.m.

The forecasts were calling for it to dump a month's worth of snow in one night.

The staff was used to such fickle conditions. They had seen it all before. The inn would be snowbound for a few extra days and there would be no comings or goings from the town below. Other than that, things would go on as planned.

They had plenty of food and drink, and a decent generator for when the power went out. Their only challenge was making sure the guests dressed extra warmly when they went out on their supervised hunting excursions.

Especially the Thanksgiving Day turkey shoot. That was known to be everyone's favourite. The hotel paid each guest twenty dollars for every turkey they shot.

They would later be served as the centrepieces of the Thanksgiving dinner.

*

Andrea Carver stood looking out of the main lounge windows like a captain on the bridge, studying a stormy sea. This was to be her first Thanksgiving as general manager of the Firelight.

At thirty-eight, she had managed substantially larger hotels, but none as renowned and as challenging as the 'Flight' as the staff referred to the inn.

It was old, but not by classic hotel standards. The big difference was the location and its occasional severance from the outside world. During storms at the hotel's altitude of almost ten thousand feet, the wind speed regularly got into the triple digits plus the temperature could stay sub-zero for months.

That sort of constant beating can take an enormous toll on a structure. Especially an old girl like the Firelight. The onsite maintenance team had to be ready to tackle urgent repairs in the middle of the night during the worst of storms.

Despite that, Andrea was looking forward to her first winter in the high Rockies. She'd trained in hotel management in Switzerland so wasn't put off by the idea of a little snow and wind.

If there was anything that creeped her out about the Firelight, it was the decor. When it was built, the owner wanted the place to not just have some of the best hunting in the country – he wanted it to look the part.

He designed the hotel to look like a huge log cabin from the outside and have the largest collection of hunting trophies in the world mounted on the inside. Every wall, every ceiling, whether in the public rooms or the guest rooms, had hunting-themed artefacts in plain view.

The Firelight was most likely the only hotel in the world that had a professional taxidermist on retainer, just to do semi-annual touch-up work. The guy was also on call in case one of the larger beasts was damaged or showed sudden deterioration.

Like New York's Natural History Museum, what was on show was only a small fraction of the whole collection.

One half of the entire basement and a good portion of the vast attic was given up to storage for all the animals and trophies.

The collection didn't just contain locally hunted varieties. It had esoteric pieces from round the globe. There was a ten-foot polar bear in the Valley View Bar. A fully intact mountain lion stood vigil on its hind legs, greeting new arrivals in the front entry lobby. The list was endless and it didn't stop at taxidermic animals. The reptile collection was equally as vast and as unnerving. At least to Andrea.

There were glassed-in cases dotted all around the hotel that contained everything from Black Mamba snakes to South American tarantulas. All dead, but they still gave her the chills.

When walking the halls at 5 a.m., as she did each day to ensure all was in order, she often felt almost intimidated by the menagerie. The guests were awed by their realism. She found it irrationally intimidating.

*

She turned away from the window just as Dave Gregory approached her. He was the deputy GM and was responsible for the unfortunately named 'Guest Affairs' department.

He looked concerned. Then again, she saw that expression from him on an almost daily basis.

"Dave. Lighten up. It's Thanksgiving," she said.

"We're missing a guest."

"Missing as in not seen recently or as in not yet arrived," Andrea asked.

"The second one," Dave nodded. "The tramway's last run is scheduled for eight thirty, so they can batten down before the storm hits. If the guy isn't on that one, he won't get up here."

"That, I am very happy to say, is not our problem. We're like a cruise ship. If the passenger misses the boat – they miss the boat."

"But this is the guy who booked the Rocky Mountain suite. We had to help with flight transfers from Denver to Vail then to Glenwood Springs. If he's late because any of the transfers were late – doesn't that make it our fault?"

Andrea studied the nervous little man and took a long calming breath.

"Have you tried calling him and checking on his whereabouts?" she asked as if speaking to a petulant child.

"Yes, of course, but our repeater is down. There's no cell phone reception at the moment."

Andrea looked at him with utter amazement. "You should have led with that piece of news. The guests may just be a trifle perturbed at not being able to use their phones while here."

"It only went down a little while ago. Ralph thinks it's probably the mule deer again," Dave stated.

"Sorry. What's one got to do with the other?" She tried to sound patient.

"They're sometimes attracted to the cell phone repeater array and like to rub their antlers on it. Every so often they knock something loose," he explained.

"Has anyone considered fencing in the array, to prevent animals from getting too amorous with it?"

She could see from Dave's expression that clearly no

one had managed such an earth-shattering idea. She wasn't sure if it was the altitude or just the local population, but there were some pretty dim bulbs working at the Firelight.

"Please ask Ralph to get up to the repeater and check it out."

"But there's a storm coming. There's not enough time to get up there and back," Dave advised. "Besides—"

"Besides what?" She was starting to lose her cool.

"If this storm's a Pineapple Express, which they say it is, then Eagles Point's gonna get ten to twenty feet of snow – easy. That much usually buries the array anyhow. Odds are we'll lose the cell and internet before midnight. There's no real point in sending anyone up there just to have it buried a few hours later."

He gave her his best toothy smile. It faded as he correctly read her expression. He lifted his walkie-talkie to his mouth.

"Ralph, this is Dave, come in. Over."

"Yo, pucker butt. What's happening?"

Dave quickly walked out of earshot of Andrea. He looked very embarrassed. He hated that nickname.

She had a momentary longing for her days back at the Grand Regency in New York. The staff there were professional, highly trained and able to think for themselves. Her job had been much easier when surrounded with people who still had fully functioning brain cells.

Andrea decided to do a quick walk-through of the catering area. The chefs hated when she did, but she didn't care. The kitchens and food storage areas were just as much a part of her purview as the public areas and rooms.

Thankfully there was one person in the kitchens who she liked and respected. Jimmy Welsh, the executive chef, was a pro. He'd also trained in Switzerland but a couple of decades before her.

She walked through the main salon then entered the Firelight Restaurant. It was breathtaking. One side of the dining room was a wall of glass that looked over the entire valley below.

She could see the lights of Glenwood Springs way below and in the distance. This was her favourite view. She liked the feeling of looking down on the world.

The restaurant was crowded as one would expect at dinner time.

She slipped through a double swing door and saw that the kitchen was in full battle mode. She was always impressed at the subtle ballet that went on in a professional kitchen. They were never big enough and the heat was beyond normal mortal tolerance level, yet somehow, in the midst of all the organised chaos, culinary artistry was created on a daily basis.

She saw Jimmy at the main grill station showing one of the sous-chefs how to get a better caramelisation on the orange roughie filets.

He sensed her presence and looked over. She gave him a questioning nod. He gave her a thumbs-up. That was about as much conversation as they ever had during service. She never wanted to disrupt the man when he was in the zone.

She walked through the kitchen and out into a good-sized service area. She went through another set of swing doors then entered a small white tiled hallway.

She opened a thick wooden door and walked into one of the biggest meat lockers she had ever seen. It had to be big. They not only had to feed hundreds of voracious meat eaters at every meal, but also had to offer meat-hanging privileges to the guests.

The front part of the locker was solely for the hotel stock – the rest of the space was for the guests. Even though most of them had only started arriving a few days ago, there were already over fifty deer hanging in the locker. Most had already been dressed but a few were obviously recent kills and were pristine except for the area surrounding where the bullet had impacted the animal.

She involuntarily shivered and stepped back out of the locker. She wasn't squeamish as such, you couldn't be in the hospitality business, but to see so many dead animals, day after day, made her feel a little uneasy.

Then again, Andrea would be the first in line for a freshly pan-fried venison steak.

She made her way back through the kitchen and headed for the tramway terminus.

Tucked away on the far side of the hotel, it reminded her of her days in Switzerland. She used to have to take an almost identical tramway every day to and from work.

She stepped out onto the concrete platform and walked as close to its end as possible. Beyond that was a sheer drop of over five hundred feet. That was just to the next ledge. The total drop from the platform to the ground station was over two thousand feet.

She stood at the safety barrier and looked down to see if the tramway was on the move. She knew it wasn't because she could still hear. When the tramway was in motion the cable retraction drum was almost deafening if you stood anywhere close to it. It was quiet at the moment.

She checked her watch. It was 8:24. Her walkie-talkie squawked.

"Andrea? It's Dave. I just got word from the ground station. We got him. He's getting on the tramway now."

"Roger that, Dave. Thank you." She was relieved.

The cable retractor suddenly fired up and began pulling the twenty-person aerial tramway up along the overhead guide cables. The noise was too much for her. She retreated back into the hotel.

As she walked towards the reception desk, she decided that she would do the registration for the last guest.

*

The staff behind the reception desk were happy to see the missing VIP appear from the tramway entrance. They had been worried that he might not make it up before the storm.

Andrea watched the young man as he approached the desk. He was not exactly a big guy. He was thin, not very tall and seemed, at least from a distance, to look kind of wimpy.

"Welcome to the Firelight Inn," she beamed. "How was your trip here?"

"Not too bad. That tramway is spectacular. I've never seen such views."

"What a lovely accent," Andrea said with a smile. "May I ask where you're from?"

The young man smiled back. "Scotland. The Highlands to be specific."

"Well I hope you have a wonderful stay here. We have some great surprises planned for the guests over Thanksgiving."

"I always like surprises."

The young man gave her a warm smile as he stared up at the giant moose head mounted on the wall behind the reception desk.

He felt the fury start to roil within him.

ALSO BY CHRIS COPPEL

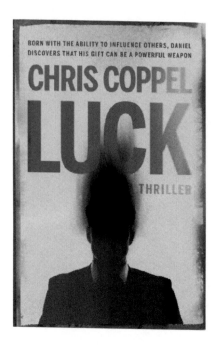

LUCK is the story of Daniel – a man born with the gift of being able to influence others. He learns that he can both charm as well as destroy. As his ability grows, so does his craving for acceptance.

Once his ability is unleashed on the American political stage, Daniel finds that he no longer has to settle with charming the few. Now he can control the minds of the masses, as his own sanity descends into a tormented oblivion.